CALICO DANCE

Alton J. Myers

4/15/13

CALICO DANCE

Escape to Sweden

Alton J. Myers

Copyright © 2003 by Alton J. Myers.

Library of Congress Number:		2003093143
ISBN:	Hardcover	1-4134-0923-7
	Softcover	1-4134-0922-9

All rights reserved. No part of this book may be reproduced or transmitted in any form or by any means, electronic or mechanical, including photocopying, recording, or by any information storage and retrieval system, without permission in writing from the copyright owner.

This is a work of fiction. Names, characters, places and incidents either are the product of the author's imagination or are used fictitiously, and any resemblance to any actual persons, living or dead, events, or locales is entirely coincidental.

This book was printed in the United States of America.

To order additional copies of this book, contact:
Xlibris Corporation
1-888-795-4274
www.Xlibris.com
Orders@Xlibris.com
19066

Author's Acknowledgments

My thanks to all, who, in any way helped
to make this book possible.
Without their help this work would never have come to fruition.

My special thanks to the instructors, who,
through their teaching in the fall of 1998
at Bowling Green State University,
inspired me to begin this writing.

PREFACE

The Protestant Reformation emerged in the sixteenth century when Martin Luther, a Catholic priest, sought to reform the Roman church. His tenets of change were more than the church could digest. Martin tried to keep within the Church but the Church could not contain what he became. The result brought a break off church. The separation was on-going with increasing numbers of people following Martin Luther and other reformers to a new worship experience.

About one hundred years later the Roman Catholic Church decided this separation had gone on too long. The loss of people, land, and church buildings exacted a great toll upon the "Mother Church." The realization of this growing loss brought conflict and financial burden, stirring the Roman church leaders to take action. They moved to stop this drain upon their resources by enacting the *Edict of Restitution.* However, the Edict produced more conflict, as many Protestants refused to come back to the Mother Church in most provinces.

In Hesse the conflict became intense. Neighborhoods fell apart over the issue of which church to stay with. People in some communities who were friends were turned into enemies of one another because of their church stance. Also the threat of invading army forces, sent to change them, forced some people to take up arms and fight against the invaders and those who sided with the invaders.

The fictional family I write about stayed Calvinist in church belief. They are forced to flee from their home in fear of opposing church factions. Life becomes so ugly in their community their only choice is to get out of town in the cover of the night time. Only a few faithful friends know of their intention to depart. The invading army finishes off any hopes they have of returning to their farm, by burning their home and taking their land.

Why this family of 1631, living in Hesse, are brought into a terrible conflict, threatening their lives, can be answered only in God's wisdom. Their purpose may be to show how strong faith can endure the worst of times and build new hopes we could never dream possible.

I write the story of their escape to describe the terror and tragedy of the day in what we now call Germany, a nation which formed in 1871, but was a set of provinces in the time of this seventeenth century conflict. Our family consists of Vater (Father), Mutter (Mother), older son John, a sister Karin and a younger sister Jutte (You'ta). The parents are near 40 years of age. The children are from their early teens to late teens. The oldest, John is a strong young man, fully grown and able-bodied, working on the farm. His sisters share quite a bit of farm responsibility also, milking cows, tending other livestock, gardening, and helping Mother in housework.

I refer to family members as Father, Mother, and the listed children's names throughout the story, which is told largely through the eyes of the three children. No family name is used. Anyone reading this story can imagine whom they wish without family bias. There are some words used in the story that would not be in the typical vocabulary of a German, in that time, but are included for the ease of modern-day American understanding.

It is not my intent to take sides in the issues of this war. Many Catholic families suffered greatly by the advances of the Protestants in this struggle. No one was immune. Whatever the church stance of the people, the cost in life and purpose was horrible to those who experienced it.

Some terms that would be helpful to know before you read this story:

Edict of Restitution—a resolution implemented by the Roman Catholic Church, March 28, 1629. The intent of the Edict was to speed up the process of returning all lands, churches and people lost in the Protestant Reformation back to Roman Catholic control. Provinces were given a specific time span in which to return to the "Mother Church." Some provinces managed to get extensions to the established return time, but most provinces who were pressured to return didn't at all, and the Thirty Years" War, 1618-1648, continued.

Elector—Much like a Landgrave except governor of a whole province.

Landgrave—a governmental leader in a province, whose religious persuasion dictated how all the other people in his territory would believe, whether that be Lutheran, Calvinist, Catholic, or something else.

Pikeman—a military man, a holdover from the Middle Ages, whose armor protected him in fighting with other pikes; the pike being an ash pole, 15 to 18 feet long. A metal point on the end of the pole was used to attack others. Sometimes it was used by horsemen, or on other occasions stationary, the pikeman standing with the base of the pole mounted to a special attachment on the inside of his shoe.

Ruffian—a reckless bandit of the day who attacked anyone along a trail who held potential as a source of food or some other treasure he wanted.

CHAPTER ONE

A warm summer breeze stirs the countryside of Hesse, Germany as Karin and Jutte wake from their sleep.

This German family, of closely knit fabric, consisting of these two sisters along with brother John, Father and Mother, are like many German families of the farm, tending cattle, working in the fields, eking out a living in this disturbed day of the Dreizig Jahre Krieg (Thirty Years' War).

Why do these people of the year 1631 have to be in this 17th century turmoil, a terrible time which pits family against family, church against church, and army against army in a talented Calvinist culture? That question is put to history lovers to answer who like to research the reason why. Whatever answer we come up with, this book will attempt to relay the message these were the times to try the life and soul of any person who set foot on German soil.

As in any day, however, the girls get up and begin to help with the chores, milking cows, while the men are feeding livestock as Mother readies breakfast. Karen, the older sister, says, "It's going to be hot today," as sweat drips from her brow. Jutte agrees as both finish with cows, collect the milk, and start for the house. The family likes farming, it's their life blood, and though it's hard work, it's what they want and hope for their future. But now a threat to their patterned lives occurs. Mother tells them as soon as they reach the house that a neighbor came over to tell her about Uncle John. He was beaten badly just two days ago because he wouldn't give up one of his cows to feed the soldiers who were passing through to join General Tilly's army to the south. Taxes upon taxes have been assessed upon the whole community, but this is the last straw. Well, those soldiers of the Catholic League got the cow anyway; it's long since been butchered and eaten despite Uncle John's efforts. Now he's on their black list if General Tilly's forces invade the area.

Karin and Jutte, on this hot summer morning, after the butter is ready and eggs are cleaned, prepare to go with their mother to trade at the village center. Their farm borders Eschwege with rows of houses near by. The horse is hitched to the wagon by Mother, and Karin gets to be at the reins. Jutte feels the air rush by, and as the wagon rolls along, she comments to Karin, "This breeze feels good."

Karin replies, "You always did like the breeze." Mother unloads the produce as they arrive at the market. Karin is trusted with the eggs, Jutte carries the butter and Mother greets the marketeer Alfred, who is glad to see them. They agree on a price. It was just a month ago that the family had an experience with their produce trade which unsettled their steady routine of farm life. No fault with Alfred, but on the way home that day they discovered they had been paid with counterfeit coins. It was too late to prove to him their loss, but it caused severe financial problems for the family. Counterfeit money was becoming a real problem in the

German countryside, and now the family watches very closely to see that Alfred reimburses them with real coins. Alfred, a good man, didn't realize what he had done the month before, and there was no way to prove his mistake to him now.

They are completely done in the next morning around the breakfast table, when they hear what Father tells them about the parson's visit last night. After all the rest of the family had gone to bed, their pastor had word, by a late night rider, that General Tilly's army of the Catholic League was advancing more quickly than expected into Hessian territory, and they had better prepare. The Papists have no love for their Calvinistic neighborhood. There's no doubt when troops arrive that the villagers will be put to the test, to defend their faith, along with the Landgrave, their village leader.

If there be a siege, there are few supplies. Not much can be kept on hand with armies taxing the neighborhood, wanting food and supplies, and certainly they must support the friendly soldiers of Hesse if they want their own protection. Even amongst their neighborhood there had been skirmishes between people siding with the wishes of the Catholic League and those who adhere to the Calvinist leanings at all cost. One family had fought another; some of their friends were involved. It was difficult for Jutte and Karin in particular, because the young people of their church had a dispute. Now, besides the bad feeling, there had been destroyed property, placing additional hardships upon the community.

Just as the family is finishing breakfast, brother John comes into the kitchen, hungry from some early morning chore duty. Midway through their conversation, the tone of what's being said hits him. His family is taut, nearly in tears. Fear, lack of supplies and now counterfeit money has all at wit's end. What to do next, with Tilly's forces bearing down on them? John blurts out an idea he has been pondering—

what role he could have to help his family and his neighborhood. Why not let him join the army? Not the Hessian army, but the invading army from the north, the Swedish army. People have been talking in the village about what Gustavus Adolphus, the King of Sweden, has been doing to help the Protestants in the north as he invades German soil. He is protecting Lutherans who ask for help; maybe he would protect Calvinists too. John has heard that he's accepting all kinds of people to be mercenary soldiers, to build his army. And there's pay, money the family needs.

Mother, Father and daughters agree in their reply, "No John, don't do it."

John answers, "But it looks like we'll be fighting anyway, to save our necks." Thoughts run deep, as the family ponders the future. They wish he would stay here, and if need be help the Hessian troops. He seems to have taken the King of Sweden as his hero. The family is slow to submit to his arguments. They love their land, the cattle, the farm, but even more they love their way of life, their culture, the tradition of hard working Germans—the family they are. Those values are much more important than the property. John rushes to the pantry to get his hands on the musket to practice shooting. The family gives a reluctant nod yes, as he begins target practice for an audition with that Swedish army a few miles away. Next day the family learns some other boys of Hesse are doing the same thing, though most are remaining with Hessian troops.

A few days later, a raid occured down the road. A farmer was shoved to the ground as a supposedly friendly Hessian soldier became violent when the farmer refused to turn over his cow for army food. Another soldier raided the kitchen pantry, stealing bread, butter, potatoes and meat from the farmer's wife, leaving her bruised and the family short of food supplies needed for their own survival. When this news reached John's family they are convinced; it is time to move north with their son, as he seeks to catch up with and join the Swedish regiment. Maybe in a few days they will be able to come back home, but for now it's just too tense here to be safe. Jutte, Karin, and their Mother look over what they have and what they need to pack into their wagon, load on horseback, or carry in their arms. It would not be good to leave anything worthwhile here; it will just be stolen, like what happened to that family down the road. At least they wouldn't be here in Eschwege, if it happens like those family friends who took quite a beating from the soldiers.

Mother and daughters move the wagon nearer to the house, on the back side, to load; they don't want disapproving neighbors to see or ask questions or know what's going on, as they ready for a secret escape from their disturbed village. Jutte carries eine Kiste (a chest) out. "No!" Mother says, "It's too heavy—we must take just a few important items; we'll have to trust other things to remain here for awhile, only what we need to travel or what keepsakes that are light and easy to load. Maybe the men can come back in a few days and collect the rest."

"You're right, Mother, I'll take only the bed linens, and some mementos—your necklace and the scarf from cousin Mary." Jutte goes back into the house to sort with sister Karin.

It's not easy, but survival is the goal, and the momentousness of the occasion sinks down upon the family. Father and John feel it too but bravely keep back emotions like many northern Germans do, to carry on in their preparations to leave. John and Father talk about the army as they ready the horses for the journey, not really knowing where they'll end up.

"Father—"

"Yes, John?"

"My friend Alex says the Swedish king leads his army in convincing fashion, with rows of pikemen mixed with following rows of musketeers and cannons. The cannons are on wheels, something we don't have here in our land. Father, I believe General Tilly will not even know what hit him when he meets up with Gustavus Adolphus' troops. In town I've heard them call the Swedish king *The Lion from the North*."

"Yes son, I've heard that too." With the horses ready, Father and son help the family quietly check things over. All is ready for the trip. A trusted friend, who does not give away secrets, will tend the cattle while they are gone.

When darkness has fully arrived, the horses are hitched, and the house secured as best can be, they climb aboard the wagon, brim full with what is needed, and start as quietly as possible toward the road. A stronger wind has picked up to rustle the leaves of the oak trees. It provides some noise to help cover the sounds made by the horses' hooves and turning wagon wheels. Jutte and Karin whisper about the stars shining brightly. A dog barks loudly as they go by a neighboring house. They fear they may be discovered and the whole escape plan thwarted. That thought runs through their minds as they huddle together in the wagon. Roll on wheels, roll on, maybe the wind with its shattering tones will cover the noise till we clear this town. Apparently it does for the dog does not wake the residents. Maybe they're used to him barking like that at some rabbit or creature of the night, at least the wheels of the wagon roll on, over the dusty trodden trail, without interruption or disruption of the commnity. The family breathes a sigh of relief that all has gone well so far.

After several hours a place is found a number of miles from their home where it appears safe to camp till morning. Now only the sounds of a soft breeze remain, as the family rests, taking turns at watch, until the breaking light of dawn invades the cover of their encampment.

Father gets up, looks out at the lay of the land. It's only another two miles to the village of Muehlhausen. There they have friends who would not turn against them or give away their secret plan of escape. The ladies could wait at their home, perhaps helping at their friends' business, a store on the village square. The men could return to Eschwege, in the cover of the evening, to see if there is any change in conditions, and rescue a few more valuables.

After a quick breakfast the family readies themselves for a visit to their friends. Off down the road, the bright sun greets them on their journey, and soon the house is in sight. In the village of Muehlhausen they find their friends, who ask what has brought them to their place on this workday. The whole family relates what has happened in Eschwege. Without further question their trusting friends accept them for this urgent stay. They will be safe here for the time being.

Later in the day Father and John ready the horses for the return trip to Eschwege. Without the wagon they will be more mobile and plans are made to bring back only limited belongings from the house. The trip will reveal to them how things are back home. Will it be safe for the family to return, while John goes on to the Swedish regiment? Late in the day, as dusk descends, the ladies bid farewell to Father and John. The trail seems shorter now, in the waning daylight, as the men leave, hoping to find their home and belongings undisturbed.

Sweden

Trelleborg

Baltic Sea

Rostock

Karow
Plau

Pritzwalk

Havelberg
Genthin

Magdeburg

Muhlhausen
Eschwege

Germany

Escape Route

CHAPTER TWO

The trees, field and sunlight all call out for tranquillity. It's peaceful here along the road in daylight. Father and John wonder, as they look at the beauriful scene of the valley before them on the trail, why there has to be war. It has really got under people's skin. It seems there is no regard for life anymore. They feel fortunate that nothing serious happened on their escape last night with family. It's well known to them how dangerous it is to travel at night. Ruffians hide at the sides of the trail ready to snatch whoever or whatever they can without respect or care for anyone's life. Father and John give thanks for one night's safety as they procede on their journey toward Eschwege.

Back at Muehlhausen the ladies discuss with their hosts what they have heard and experienced in these last few weeks of turmoil, particularly how neighbors have been assaulted by soldiers. There seems to be no end to demands and destruction brought on by the armies. They trample the fields to the extent that crops will not grow, and now food is scarce. However, now there is news of hope, if King Gustavus of

Sweden comes to their region. He brings a measure of protection which is sorely needed.

Jutte, Karin and Mother are impressed and given a ray of encouragement as their host family relates what they have heard about the Swedish King. They tell how he journeyed across the Baltic Sea, and when he with his Swedish army first set forth on German soil, he knelt and kissed the ground.

"My, that was nice of him," blurts out Jutte.

"Hush, sister," retorts Karin, "let them tell us more." Their host friends go on to say they have heard he came not to capture the land but to protect the Protestants from being overrun by the Catholic League, which is seeking to implement the Edict of Restitution.

The people of the area do not want to lose their land, their churches, their religious preference, but what can you do if you are surrounded, starving, and threatened by guns and swords? Where armies have trod for those many years, nothing grows in fields, cattle have been slaughtered by hungry soldiers. People have died, from starvation and wounds,and those who are left live in horrible conditions, especially where the fighting has been intense and prolonged. The host family gives thanks they have so far been pretty much spared, but who knows when luck will run out, and it will be their turn to resist the Catholic League and Papist forces.

"May you be spared from what we have seen," replies Mother, as she puts her arms around her dear friend.

With the day nearly over and the first hints of nighttime appearing in the eastern sky, Father and John approach Eschwege. They wonder about their home. Can they safely enter town, in the cover of darkness? The horses are tired as are they, from the long ride, but one look at the horizon with smoke rising from the valley and all else is forgotten. What's happening down there? John urges his horse forward. Father follows frantically, for the smoke looks too close to their home to be comfortable. This is trouble; they can now see smoke rising from a burning house. Entering the village John and Father see soldiers running away, and it's now clear it is their house that's in flame.

Around to the back door, they dismount and run to see if anything is still within reach before the fire reaches the interior of their home. John grabs a picture from the wall, Father finds a family Bible that was forgotten during the family's escape. Now it's too hot to do anymore, for the flames are entering the room. A couple of soldiers see them run from the burning building and go in pursuit of them. A thicket is not far away; maybe it will be protection, for it's evident the soldiers have found out who they are: the owners, who had escaped the invading forces by leaving town, the people who are Protestant rebels who undermine the Papist cause. It's people like them who have made it harder for General Tilly's forces to persuade the people to surrender to the Catholic League. Nothing left to do but burn down their house with its Protestant markings—the Celtic cross, the Bible, and other emblems of their Protestant leanings, as an example to others who may want to resist the Edict of Restitution.

But, before he can reach cover, John is caught from behind by a soldier. They struggle. Father, hiding in a bush, jumps out and hits the soldier with a rock, freeing John and him to run further into the dense bushy undercover, and away from further contact, at least for the time being. How to get the horses back is the next problem. They circle the wooded area, taking great care not to be seen by the remaining soldier, who supposes his partner is well on their trail. It's not far back to the smoldering remains of what was their home, and the horses are still tied to the tree, where they dismounted. Quietly Father and John wait as the remaining soldier becomes noticeably impatient and concerned that maybe his partner has run into difficulty. Off he goes toward the dense thicket where he last saw them. Now is their chance! John makes a run for it, while Father waits behind. To the tree, and in the darkness, lit by the few burning house embers, John unties the horses and makes his way back to Father, with both horses in hand ready for the escape.

It is completely dark now. Clouds covering the moon help to shield them from sight of other unwanted observers. Father and John lead their horses quietly through the village. Ahead is a supply wagon of Tilly's army. Everyone appears to be asleep there, or away from the vicinity. Father tells John, "There's a Catholic flag sticking out from the side of the wagon; that might be a camouflage for us in our journey." John needs no more prompting; he hands the reins of his horse to Father and tiptoes quietly to the wagon, reaches up and pulls the flag from its mooring. Nice flag, full of color, surely this will make believers of anyone they meet, that they are faithful members of the Catholic League.

Once out of the village, it's safe to begin the journey back to their family. Father and John decide to go well away from the village before they rest for the night. Along the horses go, in a slow steady trot. It's dark enough that the trail is not easy to follow. Suddenly, Father feels someone leap at him from the bushes and grab his saddle.

"John," he hollers. His son makes a leaping dismount and lands upon the ruffian who is attempting to rob them of what few possessions they were able to save from the fire—a Bible, a flag, a picture, and a small pouch of supplies. Father and John are too much for the bandit. Down he goes before he can complete his attack. He scrambles to his feet and makes off on the run for the thicket by the side of the trail, from which he had emerged.

After that shaking experience, Father and John decide

it's time to find a secure place for the night. They settle in near a grove of oak trees under the camouflage of tall grass for an uneasy night's rest. It's dark and no one will discover their horses tied there to the trees.

The rays of the morning sun shine upon them as they wake from their sleep. The clouds have disappeared, one day's journey back to family, and they should be there well before sunset. As Father and John mount their horses and head back for the trail, they feel much safer now, and talk about how glad they are that that ruffian did not show up a couple of nights ago when they were traveling with family out of the village. They decide for only daytime travel with family, if possible, for it's well known throughout the country how dangerous it is to travel at night in this German countryside, even if armies are not in the immediate area. People have become so desperate from war and lack of food that they'll attack anything.

The men approach the settlement where Mother and the girls are staying, eager to see them again, but with saddened hearts at the loss of their home and farm, which they must tell them about. Into Muehlhausen their horses gallop now. Up to the house where Jutte, Karin, Mother and friends form a welcoming party. They can tell from the men's faces that all has not been well. Once the family is reunited in the house, Father relates the unhappy news. Tears come to the ladies' eyes, for their home in Hesse is no more. All those years there with parents and grandparents has come to the fate now of so many other families, who've suffered greatly in this conflict. They who were spared for quite a few years, now suffer too. Their friendly host family offers words of comfort and what help they can for the forlorn family as they realize they must face a new life, a life away from their beloved home in Hesse.

After a night's discussion around the fireplace, Father,

Mother and children appear even more determined to continue the move northward, so they may see John enlist into the Swedish army. To them their Calvinist faith is even more important than the land in Hesse where Elector William, the Waldgrave of Hesse-Cassel will certainly face an immense struggle to keep his people in the Calvinist camp. Too much fighting, for too long, the family agrees, and quietly settles in for a fitful night's sleep before journey time tomorrow morning.

The sun comes up brightly. The family arises, nervous but somewhat refreshed. There's a good spirit felt among them as breakfast is readied by their hosts. It seems even within their grieving hearts, somehow a new life will break forth with new hope. The sunshine seems to say so, as horses and wagon are readied with what few belongings they have. The family is pleasantly surprised as their host family not only runs out to offer a fond farewell, but with arms full with food supplies to cover more than that day's journey ahead of them on their way north. They are so thankful for these kind folk who have kept them these few days. They know that neither the family on the move, nor their host will forget their meeting. Father, Mother and children promise to get word back to them somehow how the future unfolds.

Off on the trail the wagon rolls, with wheels turning up some dust as soon the village where they stayed disappears from their view. It can't be too far to the Swedish army garrison where John will meet up with his hoped-for work as a soldier. It's well known that the Swedish forces have made significant progress toward this area, meeting little resistance. Word has spread how well these troops operate, putting fear in most opponents' hearts. Who would dare to stand up to them in battle? *The Lion from the North* seems to offer significant encouragement for this family, as seemingly all else has been taken from them. John daydreams with secret anticipation, imagining what it will be like to meet up with the Swedes tomorrow. The day nears the end. The family searches for a secure place, off the trail, to spend the night. A nice thicket offers a secluded spot, and the family settles in for a relaxing night. All at once, midway through the night, John is roused as someone walks past him in tears. It's Karin.

"What's wrong?" John whispers.

"I'm thinking about our home in Hesse. It's gone," she replies wistfully.

John says, "I know," as he puts his arm around his sister's shoulder.

Karin also says, "I fear what cousin Mary will think of us, back in Eschwege. Will she call us traitors for leaving town and not staying on with the others?"

"No, I don't really think so," replies John, "After all, we've been attacked and our belongings destroyed. We'll write to her once we're settled somewhere and explain things to her." Karin, somewhat satisfied, returns to her blanket and is soon back to sleep. She is the one who usually has all the answers, but this experience has been so heart wrenching that even Karin is at a loss for what might happen in the days ahead.

Morning breaks in the eastern sky, and soon the family is back on the trail. Toward the north they go, and after traveling a few hours, a rider nears, bearing soldier gear. Father finds out he is a Protestant scout, from the Swedish garrison stationed a few miles further on. The soldier questions their purpose in travel, seeing their belongings along with Protestant emblems, flag and cross. They have hidden the Catholic flag which the men had captured, so this soldier suspects they are Lutheran. Like a calico cloth, they are able to change colors as they move. They find a new color to fit the situation, which will be a big help as they travel through this treacherous country.

Once the rider finds out their son John's intention to

become a mercenary soldier with Swedish forces, he offers to take him along to meet the Captain. Karin, Jutte, Mother and Father wish him a fond and loving farewell. John and the soldier ride off together, promising to get word back on how things go. The family waves to John as he disappears over the hill, then they start out themselves toward Magdeburg, where an uncle lives who might grant them lodging for a few days, until things are settled with John, and they have determined their future course. It's another day's journey there, but supplies should last until they reach that walled city. Uncle Thomas had visited them in Eschwege a number of years ago, and offered them a stay in Magdeburg, should they venture into that region, in the future. He is a profitable businessman in Magdeburg, and now, with this family's painful move north, it will be good to meet with this generous relative.

CHAPTER THREE

The Swedish soldier and John near the position of the garrison as they ride together into a valley. John marvels at all the cannon, and then the rows of pikemen whom he sees in afternoon drill. The soldiers are preparing to defend a village which has asked for protection, in advance of General Tilly, before the Catholic League forces have a chance to move into their village.

The soldier introduces John to the Captain, who questions and examines his fitness to be a mercenary soldier. John relates the whole story of what has happened to his family the past few weeks, and his own preparation to serve with King Gustavus Adolphus, in the cause of Protestant freedom. John shows the Captain his musket and aims it at a tree branch. He lets fire and the leaves come rippling down— a direct hit. The Captain has seen enough and heard enough; this boy is in. Off to the musket row where drill has already started, John finds his place and is welcomed into the regiment.

Father, Mother and girls travel on toward the north. So far things are peaceful with no need in the pleasant sunshine for any flags or other identity for their defense. Things have happened so fast in their lives that it's good to have some quiet time. Only the sounds of the wagon wheels churning along the trail toward Magdeburg, and the steady beat of the horses' hooves upon the soil reach their ears. Jutte dozes off on a pillow, while Karin looks across the valley's green growth, pondering what the future holds for all of them. This is beautiful. Why couldn't this quiet peaceful moment be all across this land, she thinks. But no, they are on the road for another reason, and suddenly pain interrupts their peaceful moment. Who of them can forget what happened in Hesse just a few days ago, and what is sure to happen when Tilly's forces invade the area, demanding their allegiance to the Catholic Church?

The sun is setting now, and Father, holding the reins of the horses, calls back to Mother and the girls to look in the north. There's a valley with a flowing river, the Elbe. A bit of the walled city of Magdeburg shows in distant view. All are relieved, but it's still a few miles off. They will need to find a camping spot for the night and enter the village in the morning. It's not safe for the family to travel at night. They are tired, and the horses are tired, and all give thanks for a secluded ramble of bushes, just to their left, large enough to hide them for the night.

With morning daylight, all is readied after a brief breakfast. The journey is begun into the walled city of 20,000 people. It has been a while since they've seen Uncle Thomas. Jutte and Karin barely remember his visit to them a few years back. All they can remember is his kind smile. That they will not forget, so with eager hope, the family looks forward to reaching the gate of the city. Soon they are there. The guard questions who they are, and the purpose of their visit, and off the family goes toward Thomas' house, identified to them by the description the guard gave. Down the street the wagon is pulled by horses who also seem eager, sensing that the destination will soon be reached.

There it is, the house as described by the gate guard at the edge of Magdeburg. Uncle Tom and his family are at home, and see them arrive. In a flash, he recognizes his brother's family, and all are united with hugs and warm welcome, something Father, Mother, Karin and Jutte have been looking forward to, and it seems for the moment a great burden has been lifted from their shoulders. Here are people they can depend upon for a few days. Likely they will receive supplies to start the next leg of their journey. Once they are ready and rested the journey will continue on the trail to the north. Business has been good for Uncle Tom at his store in the village, and so far no one in this town has suffered much in the conflict, quite different than his neighbors to the south. Word is, however, that Tilly's forces are headed their way, and it may not be long before things change. Father tells Tom their family's experiences, and why they have stopped, hoping for help in their escape. After all has been said, Tom understands his brother's plight and sees the reason for the move. Tom, like his neighbors, doesn't believe their walled city can be taken, yet this story of his brother brings some fear to his heart.

The family receives an extended welcome from Tom and his family. They stay there in safety for several days. Karin and Jutte are happy to get to know their cousin Elizabeth who is their age, and wish Father and Mother would decide to settle the family here, in this walled city, so all could become better friends.

Cousin Elizabeth's birthday is next month. Karin and Jutte would like to plan a party for her, but too soon all these peaceful joyful family things get interrupted by an all too familiar theme of their lives. A horseman riding into town tells what they do not want to hear. Tilly's Catholic League forces have made advances more quickly than was thought possible. Magdeburg will need to defend itself, though most people of the town don't believe anything will happen to them. Tom urges the Landgrave to call upon King Gustavus Adolphus' army for help. He tells the Landgrave that his nephew John is now a soldier in the Swedish army. Maybe the King's forces can ward off Tilly before he advances upon their city. A horseman is sent with a message of their need to the Swedish regiment, close by, but the army is occupied in defense of another community which is under siege by Tilly. It's not likely they will be able to reach Magdeburg in time to ward off an attack.

Morning breaks. Arising from a restless night, our family, including Jutte and Karin, comes to the breakfast table with Uncle Tom. All search for a peaceful day as the sun shines into the kitchen parlor. Certainly this displaced family can find comfort here with their gracious uncle, and discussion turns to John's service with the Swedish army. It's good, they say, that the officer who had met them on their journey to Magdeburg was so willing to accompany their son to the Swedish regiment. The family along with Uncle Tom awaits word of how John is getting along as a mercenary soldier. Hopefully the pay will be good to help them survive.

"You know," Jutte says, "we don't have the farm anymore, just what is in the wagon." The whole family looks at one another, thinking of their plight. It will be good to see John again.

Another day passes, and Tom's request of the Landgrave, to seek for help has an answer. The horseman who had been sent away for aid comes into town with a sad face. As most suspected, this is a busy time for the Swedish army, as many villages have requested help from this accomplished group of soldiers. Not only that, but other news from the returning horseman is not good. He had a close call in his early morning ride into the walled city. He relates that in the distance he saw what appeared to be a Catholic regiment in march toward his position, and apparently a leading scout of the troop had seen him, firing a musket at him as he reached the city gate. The horseman arrived unharmed, except for the scare of his life, and now all realize their peaceful interlude in Magdeburg may soon come to an end. Magdeburg will have to wait their turn for Swedish help. It will not come quickly.

CHAPTER FOUR

After a restless night, morning breaks, with more than just the rustling of tree leaves in the wind. It's the sound of hoofbeats, but why so early in the morning?

"Jutte," Karin shouts, "It's time to get up." Both girls wander along with their parents down to breakfast with Uncle Tom's family. Cousin Elizabeth seems afraid, a new emotion the girls hadn't noticed in her before, but all around the breakfast table they seem to sense this isn't to be an ordinary day. What about the experiences of that horseman yesterday? What he said put fear into the calmest person there. Could they really be in danger in this walled city of Magdeburg?

There's a knock on the door. Tom goes to open it, and there stands his neighbor, shaking in his boots.

"We're surrounded, Tom. Tom, we're surrounded," he repeats, his voice nearly breaking in emotion, a sight not common for this usually composed German. Tom hurries back to the breakfast table to tell them the news, but his daughter and his brother's family already know. They had heard the doorway conversation. Karin hugs cousin Elizabeth, and both begin to sob. Tom and his brother both know the siege has begun. Tilly is here; there's no escape. Their walled city is surrounded.

Breakfast is over, with hardly anyone eating the usual fare. Talk begins of what to do. Uncle Tom offers his brother's family an extended stay, until the siege is over. There's enough food, and certainly the Catholic League forces will not break into their home. Father, Mother, and daughters do not feel so confident. After all that happened to them back at their farm a few weeks before, they know the news is an ominous warning. Father tells Tom they must escape, but how, it seems already too late.

Karin says, "Father, remember that Catholic flag you captured on the way out of Eschwege? Couldn't we put it on our wagon and pretend to be Catholics who were traveling through the city?"

"Oh, daughter, quiet, it would never work, we couldn't talk our way out of this situation."

Mother replies, "Maybe we should give Karin's idea a thought. We don't have many choices if we try to escape." An eerie quiet descends upon all, as Father's family goes back to their rooms in Tom's house. The wind continues to rustle the leaves. Father hears the distant sound of hoofbeats too. It sounds all too familiar. It brings to mind what he had experienced a few weeks before, when he and son John had escaped their burning home and the rush of the soldiers who had set the fire. Somehow they had made that escape, but in the cover of darkness.

After a quiet pondering, Father calls his family together. Mother, Karin, Jutte, sit anxiously wondering what Father has to say. They have seldom seen such a grim, determined look upon his face. A hint of anger, and resolve radiates, and they know it's going to mean a commitment on their part which may test their courage. Yet, it's best, they feel, that a plan of action begin.

"Family, we are going to escape tonight. Yes, we have the Catholic flag, and it may serve as a camouflage, but our story will have to be good, for this is Saxony-Anhalt, a Lutheran province, and the soldiers will be suspicious of us."

A sense of fear, yet determination, crosses the room as the family glances at one another. All seem to sense this is the moment. All at once the sound of a musket shot rings out in the distance. Mother shouts out in almost a scream, "Yes, this is it. Father, we are with you. Jutte, get the clothes ready, there's little time left to escape."

Karin says, "But what about Uncle Tom and Elizabeth?"

Father, in an almost broken voice says, "They've decided to stay; it is their home."

Without a moment to lose, all scurry about, doing their part to load the wagon. Uncle Tom, hearing the commotion, asks his brother, "What are you doing at this late hour?" Darkness had already descended by this time.

"We're going to try an escape," Father replies.

"But it's not safe, we're surrounded by Catholic League soldiers, you wouldn't even be able to get past the city gate."

"We've got to try, Tom, my family is with me in this." Elizabeth, hearing the loud conversation, comes to the room, tears trickling down her cheek. She has just got acquainted with her cousins, and now they must leave, and in these circumstances?

Hasty farewells are said. Father, Mother, and daughters all thank Uncle Tom and Elizabeth for their generous gifts of food supplies now loaded in their wagon. They are extremely grateful for the days they have spent together in Magdeburg. Father readies the horses. Quietly out onto the street, the horses pull the wagon and family toward the north entrance of the city. Waves of farewell are given to their host relatives until darkness and distance separate them. A little moonlight helps guide their progress along the path. Musket fire is heard again: this time closer. Ahead is a soldier carrying a torch of flame. They must be nearing the gate. Karin shuffles around to the side of the wagon to straighten the Catholic flag so it will be in full view. The soldier, seemingly unimpressed by their Catholic camouflage, says, "You can't get through the gate."

Father doesn't challenge him, but rather turns the wagon down a side path; surely there's another way out of here. Scared daughters and Mother cling to the sides of the wagon as Father hurries the horses. Houses look gloomy in the night, as though pending a dire situation soon to happen. People are in hiding or already in bed. Ahead the family sees a second gateway out of the city that appears unattended, at least for the moment. In an eerie calm, Father turns the horses in the direction of the gate.

Karin shouts, "Look!" A big ball of flame appears behind them, almost in the same vicinity they left a few minutes before.

"What happened?" Jutte cries out to the others in the wagon.

"It's a house," says Father. "Remember the man with the torch? Someone has done something to provoke him, I suppose, and it doesn't look good. We'll have to hurry through the gate, even if it isn't the road we want. Musket fire breaks out again, and people are running from their houses now, in the dark of the night. The family reaches the gate, but there's a wooden barricade preventing passage. "So that is why it's unattended."

Everyone jumps out of the wagon, lending a hand to remove sticks and logs as best they can. Just enough space now to get through, when up rides a horseman, a Catholic League soldier, who asks them what they're up to.

"We're just passing through town, we stopped for the night, but since we have supplies and there's turmoil here, it's best we move on."

"I see you're one of us, so move on your way."

Father, Mother, children give a sigh of relief, and thank God for their Catholic flag. They prod their horses to start down the trail, outside the city. It's a different trail than they had planned, but at least it's a chance for life. Just a few more strides, and they look back—a second house is on fire and there, a soldier strikes a person on the street who falls to the ground. There are soldiers now all over. Have they come away from just a siege? No! It's more than that. It's a battle now, and soldiers are entering the town.

Jutte whispers to Karin, "We've made it just in time. Perhaps another soldier wouldn't have believed us, and we would be back there fighting for our lives." There are more screams, the city is being raided. Soldiers are now carrying away house supplies, food, clothing—whatever they can get their hands on. People are being beaten on their heads with muskets and tools whenever they resist.

Our family moves straight ahead, afraid to look back. They can't wait to get further away from the noise and the cries of hopelessness. It's death repeated again. It's a familiar chord chiming in their lives. The horses keep plodding along too, like they know what our family is feeling. All are eager to get away from here.

It's rather dark now—just the glow from the distant burning houses helps lighten the path enough to keep going a little further. More musket fire urges them on. Someone in the city is returning fire upon the soldiers. The battle is getting worse.

CHAPTER FIVE

On down the road they go; though they are now some distance from town, why is it light? Mother glances back, "Oh, no, the whole town is on fire." Everyone in the wagon trembles with fear. What about Uncle Tom and Elizabeth, they're still back there, and there's nothing we can do for them. The smell of ash and smoke reaches their nostrils as the wind has shifted. The smell is horrible; dead people on the street, they think. No way to get over those walls, and soldiers block the gateway, so people there are trapped in a raging inferno. Tears for their relatives and all the people back there in Magdeburg, distant screams still reach their ears as Father searches the roadside for a place to spend the night. There, to the left is a thicket. We can hide there in safety from any thieves or ruffians. Jutte and Karin jump down from the wagon and begin to unload needed items for the night. It's an eerie feeling, but those bushes look like an inviting place! Safety is what this family seeks, as Father moves the horses and wagon a little further off the trail, well hidden by the tall grass and branches.

Somehow, after all is taken care of, they relax, a forced relaxation from overly tired bodies lulls them to sleep, with the sound of distant musket fire still in their ears. Karin is aroused in the middle of the night. Just enough awake to hear the sound of footsteps—out of the corner of her eye, without a motion or a sound, she sees what she doesn't want to see, a soldier, sitting down for a rest, and he's close enough to hear him whisper to his partner as both converse before marching on toward Magdeburg. Their uniforms are visible through the branches, and the nearer one has medals on his chest, he must be an officer. Karin nearly holds her breath, praying her family will not be discovered there in the thicket. A few more moments and the two men pick up their muskets, after their brief rest, and continue their trek toward the fire lit site of what was Magdeburg. Karin breathes a sigh of relief, giving thanks the rest of her family slept quietly through this whole incident.

A hint of light appears in the east; it's nearly dawn, and Father is up to ready the horses for the journey before daylight reveals their position. Breakfast can wait until they are further away from this horrible scene. Jutte straightens the Catholic flag on the carriage. making sure it's fully visible while they are yet in the environs of the Catholic League forces.

Soon off they go down the trail, with the smoke of burnt-out Magdeburg, once again in their faces, as a morning breeze picks up. It's horrible as they think of all those people back there, who never had a chance in that wall of fire spreading through their homes. It's then, that Karin relates her midnight vision of soldiers marching so close to their encampment, and all realize how fortunate they were not to be discovered. The family gives thanks for divine protection through that night and looks forward to a hoped-for reunion with son John.

Father knows of a village ahead which is east of where

they want to be on this less-traveled path. It will have to do for now, it's just too dangerous to work their way back to the main route. The Catholic League is on the advance there and their Catholic camouflage might not last through a full inspection by the league officers. Karin and Jutte look through their food supply to prepare a lunch on the road as in the distance a vision of Genthin appears. Mother, after a nap, awakes to help serve. Father, eating and driving the wagon, gives a sigh of relief; it seems they have successfully cleared the Magdeburg area and now can lower the Catholic flag and pretend to be Lutheran again. Wheels roll on raising dust, it's good to hear Karin in laughter, as Jutte rolls up the Catholic flag to sit on. It cushions the bumps of the jolting ride. Rocky road, you'll not do us in, we've handled worse things than you.

Genthin, here we are. The sun is now low in the sky, and Father finds a house where chores are going on, cows being milked. He asks the farmer about lodging if the family would share in the work of the farm for a few days. Somehow all clicks; a bargain is reached, and a tired family finds a place to regain their strength, replenish their lives and prepare for their continued journey,—meanwhile—John, the family's son is fully in Swedish uniform, serving faithfully in King Gustavus Adolphus's army, unaware his family is staying in a village a few miles south after their harrowing experience in Magdeburg.

It's morning, and the troops are moving out toward Rathenow, which has fears of the Catholic League encircling their village in siege. They have called for the Swedes to assist, so they may retain their Lutheranism. John follows the pikemen, in the row of musketeers. He is now a well-trusted soldier having responded marvelously in the one battle of last week in Anhalt-Saxony. He would like to meet the Swedish king, his hero, but John knows that' s a slim chance.

One of the pikemen speaks to him about his experience in defending the King in one of the attacks a couple of months ago. John is all ears as he drinks in every detail of the event like a deer listening for an approaching hunter.

It's near noontime and word has come through the line of men, to be prepared for a coming encounter with lead troops of the Catholic League. Some scouts have reported sighting cannon over the hill, near the village they are called to protect. John knows this means action soon, for those cannon are right in the path where the Swedes must march.

Kaboom! All at once the Swedes are forced to take cover in a wooded area. The Catholic League has discovered them, and now it will be a challenge to set defense for the village, still two miles away. Fortunately, no one was hurt in that first cannon blast, but muskets are blazing now and the armies come near. John, and some other soldiers, including the pikeman he had just talked to, are assigned special duty of going around back of the advancing league to surprise them in the rear. John wonders if this may be a plan of the Swedish King himself, as all soldiers in this special assignment, circling though the woods, are of the highest caliber, intent on succeeding in this task. John has heard how the King is able to inspire his men to accomplish great things. The soldiers march toward a valley where the rear of the Catholic forces are reported to be. In the sunlight a shiny object appears on a distant ridge; over toward a thicket. The men approach, careful to stay hidden from the unexpecting troops who think all the Swedes are ahead of them.

It's best to wait until sunset or later to make an attack, and all hope, including John, that the armies can be kept in check until this opportune time, to launch a surprise assault.

That shining object, now glistening in the setting sun, is now close enough to be seen as the outline of an armor-bearing soldier of the Catholic League. John laughs softly, thinking how cumbersome it is to still be fighting a war in that gear, as muskets are replacing most older types of warfare of the Middle Ages. The Swedes do have the most modern approach, and it paid off in winning a number of battles against the unprepared Germans, who are baffled by the power of *The Lion from the North*.

John and the rest of the select soldiers have completed their advance by sunset, and launch a volley of shots in the valley. The surprised Catholic League forces scurry for cover, not wanting to engage them this near to twilight. The plan has worked, and Swedes pass them by and head toward the village which has requested protection. There are a few mock attacks by scouts of Catholic forces hidden in the bush, but they are resoundly rebuffed and recede. The pikeman ahead of John defends him in one encounter, and John in turn has opportunity to fire upon one armored man who had turned upon his pikeman friend. Into the village for the night, the Swedes are greeted by friendly villagers who offer them food and drink. John really likes his work now, and is feeling very comfortable around his Swedish friends as all settle down for well deserved rest. Soon the rest of the troops will be able to join them now that a pathway has been secured.

It is the next day when John sees his life change in fabulous ways. Yes, the village is secured, waiting to see if Catholic forces try a raid. If they do, the villagers know they have the Swedes to back them up. In that sense, things seem more calm for them, and John appreciates a chance to talk with some of the Swedish soldiers. Here comes the Captain. John was first introduced to him when he joined this Swedish regiment. During their talk, John finds out it would not be difficult to become a Swedish citizen and receive more pay, an extra help for his family. John tells the Captain he would like to become a Swede, and there on the spot it happens, as the Captain pulls out a book, gives John the details. An oath is taken, and John is a true Swede. What a day; now if only he could meet his hero, the Swedish King, his life would be fulfilled. Dusk comes after a day of patrolling the village. The Captain knows John's wish to see the King, so as officers gather to plan the future defense work, it so happens there's a need to have someone deliver a message to Gustavus Adolphus about supplies and other information of the regiments. John nearly jumps out of his boots as he is selected to go on horseback to the nearby location of the King, to fulfill that task. He eagerly accepts the responsibility, readies his horse, and with papers in hand takes off to do his task.

He is greeted by officials and identifies his mission to see the King. Off to a special area, through the door of a home, there the King is resting, as news of an eager messenger is announced. John receives a handshake from King Adolphus as he turns over papers from the Captain of his regiment. The King asks John to sit down as a reply will be readied to send back. John looks at the King in awe, as decisions are made with officers huddled around the King. What a stately man, John thinks, as his eyes remained focused upon his hero, there in full battle uniform though he is a King of a country, What a brave man he is; John ponders why would he risk himself to come in these German provinces, as a protector of Lutheranism? It is truly awesome for John to share these moments in his presence, now a Swede himself, looking at his King. With all his success, winning battles, John realizes why people call him *The Lion from the North*, especially so when swiftly the King rises and slaps new papers into the hands of John for delivery back to his garrison. There's a sincere smile from the King that nearly wilts the heart of John. Up from the chair John rises, turns toward the door and with shivers running down his back heads for his horse, filled with hope for this desperate land. He had not felt this way for months. It was long before this war had touched his family's life, that anyone had any hope in this land, and bit by bit it had been lost until King Gustavus Adolphus invaded these German states.

The ride back to the regiment is pleasant, and though the Catholic League forces are nearby, somehow John knows things will turn out all right. Listening to the steady hoofbeats of his horse, John begins to wonder how his family is doing in their frantic journey away from Hesse.

CHAPTER SIX

Back at Genthin John's family is doing well, with all four working hard in support of their host family. It has been nearly two weeks here with this Lutheran family, and Karin's thoughts, typical of all four of them, are upon her brother, as she says "Do you suppose John is nearing this area?"

Jutte says, "I think he is, it seems so to me, we will be together soon, I know it." Those are thoughts of the whole family who seems to be protected in their Calvinistic faith.

The next morning they are awakened by the sound of hoofbeats on the ground outside their host family's house. It's early but they can hear the horseman conversing with the men of the village who have gathered to meet this contingent, who turn out to be advance scouts of the Swedish army. Father calms the family as all run to him to find out what's going on.

Jutte says, "Father, what's going on? Are we safe here, or is it time to plan an escape?" Nerves are torn, by weeks and weeks of upheaval this displaced family has felt, first hand, in the war-torn German states from which they come. Father reassures them, and with the quickness of the morning breaking light, goes out to find an answer to his family's questions.

Father is greeted by the farmer who is their host, and together they join the men of the village who are listening to the message of the horsemen. Father soon finds out these are advance men of the Swedish forces who are asking if the village will request help, in defending themselves, as General Tilly and his Catholic League men approach their area.

This upbeat community has heard about what happened in neighboring communities who tried to go it alone. They do not want their community to be put under siege. They know their Elector does not have enough troops to protect everyone who seeks to hold fast to their Lutheran faith and practice; so the answer is yes, we need the Swedish King to help us through this time. *The Savior of Protestantism* is what King Gustavus Adolphus has become to be called by quite a few religious people of this time, and after his decisive victory at Breitenfeld there was no doubt of his ability even among the Catholic League people.

Father approaches one of the soldiers to ask if he knows his son John, who is a mercenary soldier with the Swedish army. After a detailed description, the answer is yes, I know him, he has served well, even delivering the King's orders to our regiment, on horseback last week. Your son is not a mercenary any longer, he has become a Swedish citizen, serving as one of us. Father inquires whether they might see him when the garrison comes in protection of Genthin. "Quite likely" comes the reply, "I will let him know his family is here, in this place. I think the officers can arrange such a meeting, perhaps assigning him duties that will put him near your location."

Good news to all the family, for soon they feel, John will

be in their midst. Karin and Jutte go about their morning duties, glad their Father has talked to a soldier who knows John.

"Karin," says Jutte, "I wonder if we'll be able to leave this town without a fire, I never want to see another Magdeburg, my heart aches for Uncle Tom and his family and all those other town people, back there."

"Yes," Karin replies, "we've seen enough, I just hope the Swedes get here in time, before General Tilly can begin a siege around Genthin."

Next day the sound of hoof beats awaken the townspeople as the Swedes arrive. Shouts of joy ring out in the crisp morning air as the whole town gives thanks the Swedish King has responded in time. Their prayers have been answered, the Swedes have arrived ahead of the Catholic League. The local menfolk gather up guns and swords, offering to help in whatever way may be needed, while the women collect the food and other supplies the soldiers will need for a protracted stay. Father and Mother are happy to see the soldier who knows John, and they run from the house to meet him. He remembers his talk with Father, and points to an incoming row of horsemen bearing muskets. It's John, they recognize him from a distance, no doubt their son will be right here in Genthin, for a least a few days.

As soon as all horsemen are accounted for, an officer approaches John, gives him permission for a short leave, to be with family, while the other soldiers begin preparations in defense of the village. By this time Karin and Jutte, having finished morning duties with the host family, run to the scene to see what Father and Mother are up to. It doesn't take long to find out what all the clatter is about, for right there before their eyes, brother John is running to meet them all. Hugs, smiles, and joy radiate among family members, who have had little to be happy about in these past months. John tells them he is all right and thriving in his choice to serve in the Swedish regiment. Together, they chat, as all of them head back to their host family's house.

Feeling more secure under the protection of Swedish troops, the family's discussion with John turns to questions about his past weeks' experience as a soldier. John's first pay, in Swedish talers is in his army gear. As he reaches to share coins with his family, to help in securing supplies for their future journey, he relates that he is now a Swedish citizen. He has found good success in his garrison, and now, having chosen to be one of them, as a Swede, will have even more chance to progress in service and stature for his new country.

The family is shocked to find out of John's decision to become a Swede, and ask what moved him to such a step. It was the excellence of their planning, the way they could anticipate the battle, and handle the challenge, I was in awe, he says. John goes on to tell of his one meeting with King Adolphus, and though it was a brief encounter he sensed the good purpose in the man. "You know," he says, "I've never experienced so much optimism before. Yes, I love our German tradition, but look what has happened to us. We need some optimism for our days."

Karin and Jutte nod in favor of his decision, and look in wonder at the beauty of the day's sunshine as they think about their escape from Hesse and burning Magdeburg. Even though the sun is hot in the burning drought of summer, with all the dust around, they sense a change for their lives which may produce hope. Through the heat, God's Spirit works, despite their troubled days. There's a sense of God's providence working among them, Father and Mother sense it too. Together, the family looks over their supplies. They will need to buy some things, helped by John's pay, before they start out again. The money does offer hope, a bit of good to think about. Their son a Swede, and they without a home, the home that was theirs for generations in the German state of Hesse. Are they nomads wandering about as so many peoples are in this wartorn countryside? Father looks longingly at Mother. Both realize they need a plan. The family is at stake; they need safety and a purpose. Is John their example?

The evening is a time for parting, for John must get back to his garrison. After supper they say their farewells but sense it may be a new beginning. Starting out will mean separating further from John, for now, but in their travels, hopefully, they can keep out of harm's way amidst the battling countryside of the German states they're escaping. Now they have some purpose to think about, in John's good treatment amongst the Swedish soldiers.

Karin and Jutte help Mother and Father round up belongings, before bedtime, as likely tomorrow will be a good time to leave this area before a possible siege or battle happens, with the arrival of Catholic League forces. Resting is more comfortable this night, knowing John is happy and doing well in his role as a soldier. There are hopes the family can reunite again, later on, somewhere along their escape route, for this is the promise they made when John left to return to his post amongst his Swedish brethren. Karin says to Jutte, in the night just before sleep overtakes them both, "What would it be like if we became Swedes?"

"I don't know," says Jutte, "but it would sure be different from what we are now."

John, back in the garrison, is greeted upon his return with news that their work will soon start, for General Tilly's lead soldiers have been sighted advancing toward Brandenburg. It's good they have become prepared, ready a full day ahead for their defense. There's a feeling of confidence, General Tilly or any other army will have a difficult time if they choose to advance against this well-trained unit of Swedish soldiers. In this comfort, John falls back on his bed ready for a relaxing night's sleep before a taxing day tomorrow in defense of Brandenburg. He feels good he has told his family of his experience, and hopes they too can find a purpose in their escape from Hesse.

It's the middle of the night at the host family's house. The family is awakened by the stirring of Father. He has reached a decision, perhaps in an early night dream, but it's clear to him what they must do. And the news is too important to keep till morning. Sleepy eyed Karin rouses Jutte. "What's going on? Are we being attacked?" Jutte emits in a half-dazed voice.

Karin says, "I don't think the Swedes have our village surrounded. Troops couldn't get through that easily, but Father is up, and he wants us together by the fireplace." Soon all four are there. What is it, Father? Are you sick? No, my family, it's a decision that has become clear to me, and I want to see how you feel about it, before I think it out further.

"What is it?" Karin says.

"Well, I believe our plan must be in line with what John has done. We're nomads now, just wandering further from our home that is no longer there in Hesse. Our community is crushed, and I've lost my only brother in the Magdeburg fire. We have each other, the five of us, but we need a place of peace, a place where life can be lived with some sense of security. John has told us things that rest heavily on my mind."

"Let us know what it is," replies Mother.

"It's a new country," Father says. We need to head to the north to escape the advancing army of Tilly and Wallenstein. We might as well seek our way toward Sweden, maybe by some way we could make it to that country and start a new life; John is already a Swedish citizen, perhaps that is the future we can find with him."

Smiles appear on everyone's face. They all are feeling the same way, though the word had not been spoken until now.

With that calming thought, now verbally expressed, all return to finish the night's rest—dawn is not far away. With the mystery of a new day's traveling ahead of them, Karin and Jutte, Mother and Father give thanks the family is together on this. A welcomed rest refreshes them for the remainder of the night.

CHAPTER SEVEN

Morning breaks with a clean bright glow in the eastern sky. The sun seems especially bright as the family rises from a good night's rest. Our family knows it will be hot again this late summer day, and and all wish for cooler weather for their ongoing journey. Maybe that will happen soon as they travel north, but more important is their escape from Genthin before trouble happens here. Their host family is up early too, wondering how things are going outside their village where army protection is already in place. Father greets his host with news of their night's decision to move on to the north, today, before there may be conflict with Tilly's force. The host family understands their concern and agrees it would be wise for them to start their journey today, unless they would like to stay on and become inhabitants of their town.

"No! We really like it here, and you people have been so nice to us, but our plan is to reunite with John, later, in our northward journey toward the Baltic coast." These words are said by all the family, around the breakfast table, each in their own way. The host family will miss them, for they had not only become good friends, but shared in the chores and duties of the household, proving to be very good workers.

"We understand," is their host's reply, "but know that you're always welcome here, among us Lutheran folk. We're not going to give in to the Catholic League, our Elector has assured us of that. The Swedes will protect us in our decision."

After expressing thanks, Father, Mother and family begin loading the wagon with help from their hosts, who add a generous food supply to their cargo. Horses are ready, the family is assembled, the journey begins with waves of goodbye. The family realizes they have made true friends, and should they decide to return, in case something goes wrong, they have a place they would be welcome.

With the journey underway, through the village outskirts, the family finds the road to the north. Meeting little resistance on the way, except for some questioning from Swedish troops in place there, they feel a sense of assurance in this yet undisturbed countryside with hope for a good day's travel. It is a long way to the Baltic coast, but at least they will be moving away from the present conflict areas. The family is relieved to have the additional supplies they have been given, and for the first time in many weeks a more restful, uneventful life is theirs as they progress from village to village northward, over the next several days.

Meanwhile, John's experience grows as a Swedish soldier, having left Brandenburg without a conflict, as Tilly backed off from there, at least for the time being. He thought the Swedish garrison too strong for any assault upon the town. John continues to mature in experience, being promoted in rank, with more responsibility in planning. The elite Swedish garrison, of which he is a part, is called from village to village to answer requests from Lutherans to be protected from the penetrating Catholic

League, which does not compromise easily in enforcing the Edict of Restitution. Most of the time John's work is in organizing positions, to prevent the opposing army from setting up a siege, but sometimes there is open conflict when the enemy brushes up against them. His role then can shift from musketman to pikeman and back as need exists. The severity of the conflict determines his place with the soldiers available. He does well most any place he is called.

John hears of his family's departure from Genthin with a note arriving through a horseback rider, relaying their intent to make for the Baltic coast. The note is from the host family, whom he had met in his brief visit at Genthin several days before. He hears of their decision to seek out the Swedish country as a possible residence. A sense of joy settles within him, for he feels it is a good decision, which will unite his family for a new beginning outside this horrible conflict. John knows the King's movement will likely take him north as defense of villages continues. The possibility looms strong that he will be able to rejoin family again before they reach the Baltic coast.

Village to village the family moves until supplies run low. "Father," Karin says, "are we going to stop in a village soon, that will welcome us for a few days of rest and new food to eat?"

"Yes, my dear, your Mother and I have been talking about the same thing, and we will be in Havelberg by evening if things go well today. I know a family there who has moved from our area in Hesse, ten years ago, to continue their trade as tailors in a shop there. I know they could help us for a few days."

"That sounds good." replies Jutte. "I'm really tired, we've been traveling day after day for quite a while, but I am glad we haven't been attacked."

"Yes," Father says, "I'm happy about that too."

The day moves along, in that flat northern German countryside. It's sunny today, brightening the hopes of the family, that the next village will welcome them as well as the last. It will be good to rest for a few nights in a home, rather than camping in underbrush for each night's sleep, where there was always fear of ruffians or unfriendly animals finding their position. As evening nears, the village of Havelberg comes into view.

The family reaches the village before sunset and begins inquiries about their tailor friend's clothing shop. "It's right down the street," comes the reply from a seemingly friendly man who greets them like they were not strangers, but friends. It soon becomes evident that anyone who knows their tailor friends, of the clothing shop, are friends of the community, even if the community has not before seen these strangers who are entering their town.

Karin says, "I like the way that man greets us, with a smile, as soon as we mentioned the name of our friends of the clothing store."

A warm welcome comes as soon as the family enters the store, for it has been ten years since this tailor left Hesse, to take up business in Havelberg, and nearly everyone has had business with him joyfully in this village. They are accepted for a couple days' rest, and as night falls, Father, Mother and daughters begin to tell their long story to their tailor friend of how they escaped Hesse, Magdeburg and other places along the way in fire and siege.

There are hugs and tears, as they settle in for a comfortable night's rest with their gracious hosts. However, in the back of everyone's mind there's an awesome fear that it may not stay this way, for there are rumors Wallenstein may be advancing this way in a northern route. It is a three-pronged attack, by not only the Catholic League, but by emperor too, as the Hapsburg family wants to retain a hold upon the area. The Swedes are yet far to the south, so it will be up to this province to protect itself from Wallenstein, and perhaps Tilly too, eventually, as the war progresses. Maybe there will be some help from the forces of the Protestant alliance, but so far it has been a loosely knit group, not too dependable.

As morning breaks, Father and Mother call their daughters down to breakfast. All had a good night's rest, and a very welcome smile is on everyone's face, as talk centers on plans ahead. It seems good to our family to have gotten this far along on their journey toward the port city of Rostock, but they do hope to rejoin son John before that destination is reached. Their tailor friend encourages them to take some time here, before they return to the trail.

Mother watches as the skilled fingers of the tailor finish an article of clothing for the shop that day, and soon finds herself joining in the task of sorting items to help the shop owners. Karin and Jutte decide to stay at the house to prepare food and meals for the day, then go to the shop itself, to see how a tailor works. Father is out about town, learning about the people and the area around, when a horseman rides into the village. News circulates quickly through the village that this horseman, who is a fur trader, has seen evidence of an army on the move some miles from their town. Everyone wonders what this means, could they be in danger in this province, which so far had not entered into conflict?

The next day their question is answered, as the tailor comes running into the house following the morning breakfast, to give news our family doesn't like to hear. That army advancing is Wallenstein. "He's moving our way," the tailor says, almost in tears.

"Oh, no!" Karin shouts, "not more of this!"

Jutte says maybe that horseman was wrong, maybe he mistook their identity, and thought they were soldiers. "I'm afraid not, Jutte," says the tailor. "A second horseman, an army scout, has been seen just a mile from our village, asking questions and demanding food for him and his horse. He'll be in our village by noon, searching us out, whether we'll support them or reject their cause. There's no way out of meeting with him."

Father looks grimly at Mother. The smiles of that early morning have slipped from their faces, for this sounds too much like Hesse, Magdeburg, and a host of other villages before. The whole family feels their hearts melt, as they remember all those close calls. The need for action crosses all their minds. Like trained warriors, they churn through the events they have experienced. They are not official soldiers, nor do they understand the techniques of battle, yet they have seen enough to know the forewarnings of danger, from the youngest, Jutte, to their Father, of more mature years.

Father pauses, then with a firmness in his voice, gentle but sincere, speaks to his gracious tailor friend, before it's off to a day's work. "Morgen, we've really appreciated all you have done for us, but today we must pack and ready ourselves to journey on, for I fear this area too will see the ravages of the conflict. I hope this doesn't happen here, but the news you've just told us brings fear to my heart. Our family has experienced too much to be put through more, and I think it's best for us to move on before forces come to seek out your village. I hope your people can retain your Lutheran faith, without the compulsion to give in; that your Landgrave will hold firm, but you know it's you people who will have to hold out. The Swedes are too far away to help now, but maybe you can find a way to stall off Wallenstein until help arrives."

More tears fall from Morgen's eyes as he readies some material for his shop. "I understand," he says. "Be careful today as you load your wagon, I don't want to put fear in our neighbor's hearts, or cause them to question why you are preparing to leave. We need all our townspeople to remain here in defense, and if they hear of your experiences they may flee."

"Yes," replies Father, "we will be careful and not let on there is any trouble brewing."

"I'll let you know this evening of any news I learn today at the shop when Wallenstein's scout comes to town."

"Thanks, Morgen," Father nods, and the family quietly goes back to search out what they will need for the journey. The family goes about its tasks in anticipation of a difficult day.

Karin says, "I wonder how brother John is getting along, I think he sees even more tension than we do."

"Sure," says Jutte, "but he's trained and knows how to defend himself a lot better than we do, and with all that help of his garrison, he has a lot better chance than than we do, if there's fighting."

"Now, now, children, "Mother replies. "Your Father has a good plan for us, we'll get through tomorrow okay. Yes, I'm sure John is doing fine, and we'll be fine. I think we'll see John again before too many days, as we journey north, for we know King Gustavus Adolphus will return to this area with his troops when his work is done in the villages we've come through."

That reassurance seems helpful, and the day goes along better for this family in their preparations. At supper, that night, their tailor friend relates his day's experience with the horseman scout who arrived in town. Morgen, with a worried face says, "He's questioning us about how we believe, and whether we'll willingly return to the Catholic faith. I'm afraid he's not willing to compromise or leave us alone, for he knows he has a whole army out there ready to force us to change to the Catholic tradition of faith and worship if we're not willing to do it on our own."

"I can see why you're worried," replies Father. "Your Landgrave is a strong Lutheran, and I'm sure he will not be willing to compromise his faith, let alone change it. The family now senses they'd better be ready for an early departure in the morning, for they do not want to get caught up in another tragic conflict like they went through in Magdeburg. That scout of Wallenstein remains in the village all night, along with some other troops who come in support of his mission. They go from house to house now, seemingly more irritated at the response they are getting. The family hears some shouting going on. They rest uneasily as they wait for the glimmer of dawn in the eastern sky. This village is not as peaceful now as when they arrived, and it is apparent a strong spirit of determination will remain within this German community, to defend their church and belief to the end, whether it's by siege or by battle. The Catholic League will find a tough struggle trying to regain this northern German countryside, especially when they are being weakened by the strong impulse of the Swedish King in their homeland area to the south.

Fear, instead of peace, enough is enough, and our family in this restless night of sleep, subconsciously becomes even more determined to reach the Swedish shores, away from all the horror going on in their Hesse homeland and the other provinces of these German people.

CHAPTER EIGHT

When morning finally breaks, our family is up early, finishing any packing of things into the wagon before neighbors are up to see. An army scout rides up to the door of the tailor's house, and our family hears the conversation, as they finish breakfast. It is not good. The Wallenstein scout is angry. He wants supplies: clothing for the Catholic troops. Morgen refuses, and the scout shoves the tailor up against the wall. Our family looks on in horror. Finally the tailor agrees to give him something out of the closet, but words are exchanged, and the conversation is that this town does not have long until it will be invaded. The scout has found no co-operation whatsoever among these strong Lutheran folk of the village.

When things calm a bit, our family from Hesse readies for the trip, says farewells to the trembling tailor, wishing him well in what they know will be a dreadful time. How will they escape, is the next question, for certainly they will be seen and stopped by the number of Wallenstein troops already on the streets? They have that Catholic flag in the back of their wagon, stolen in the beginning of their escape journey weeks ago in Hesse, but it would not go well to hoist it now, in the presence of these Lutheran villagers. All Aboard! The horse starts out, pulling the wagon and the family down the street, past a row of houses. Our family seeks to act out a role of just going to the market place, saying hello to people who are watching them pass. When on through the village they go, leaving the market place in the dust, suspicions arise, and one of Wallenstein's scouts takes after them.

"Where are you going?" comes from the soldier.

"We're one of you. We didn't want the villagers to know," as Karin reaches to the side of the carriage to bring out the Catholic flag, which was well hidden there for the past several weeks. Father helps to hoist it to the top of the wagon as Jutte lends a hand to fasten it in place.

"This is what we like to see," replies the army scout, as he quickly gives his assent for them to travel on out of the village.

"Wow!" echoes Karin, "That was a close one. I am so glad we've kept that flag; I just hope the news doesn't get back to our village hosts, that we've turned color on them in order to escape. They would really be angry with us if they knew we pretended to be Catholic to save our skin."

"Yes," replies Jutte, "they were nice people, I wouldn't want to lose their friendship; it's too bad they have to remain back there in a possible siege or attack." The family breathes a sigh of relief as the village disappears in the background, for the road ahead now looks good for them. This is a dance of many colors, if you want to get out of this German countryside alive, and our family is learning to do it well. As evening reaches the western sky, Father decides they can put up for the night, now safely away from the area Wallenstein is concentrating upon for now. Karin helps to take down the Catholic flag, Jutte puts in back in a hidden place of the wagon. A sense of their Calvinist background returns to their hearts as they settle in for a good night's rest.

With morning, the trail resumes to the north toward Pritzwalk. A bright morning sky brings encouragement. The sound of singing birds in the nearby trees leaves a peaceful feeling this family has had little of, in these past few months. Karin and Jutte are actually singing as the wagon moves along, however near lunchtime an object moving toward a fork in the road catches their eye. Karin shouts to Father, who is busily handling the reins, "Look over there, across the field; I think I see another wagon that looks a lot like ours, and they are going to join us soon, as the road meets with ours."

"You're right, Karin, I see them too. I hope they are friendly, not a load of ruffians we'll have to deal with."

In a few short minutes the two groups meet, right where the roads come together. Our family gives a sigh of relief, for it soon appears this is not a load of ruffians, but another family much like themselves. As they stop to talk, our family finds out these people are also escaping from a village in conflict that was hit by Wallenstein's forces about a week before the attack on Breitenfeld. Their story is a sad one, paralleling much of what has happened in our family's escape from Hesse. Farmland trampled, cows stolen, people starved in seizure, death and destruction, brought on by army forces who have become calloused to any meaning of life other than their own survival. There's no end to it, this new family says. Our family agrees; it's hopeless, the only course is to leave, and hope to arrive safely somewhere else.

The two groups share lunch together, and as they talk, the decision is reached to caravan together, at least for now, as both groups are moving north. The idea is a good one, for it will bring added safety in the wilds of the country, to be together, whatever the road is like ahead.

The afternoon travel continues well. Jutte joins the new family's wagon to get acquainted with their daughter, her exact age, and they quickly become friends. Karin helps Mother rearrange some things in the wagon as they prepare for the yet long trip to the port at Rostock, but with more assurance now as they travel in caravan with this new and hospitable family.

As evening approaches, Jutte returns to tell Karin and the rest of her family some interesting details about their new traveling companions. They're Lutheran, although not apparently strong in their church attachment. Jutte relates how the soldiers had no respect as their village was stormed, ripped of most of its resources, with many of the people left to die. Jutte says, "They're like us in many ways except for the church, and I believe we can trust them as our friends for these few days of travel."

"You know," Father says, "we don't want to tell them now of our plans to leave the country, better to put that off till later, when we know them better."

"Yes," Jutte agrees, "I'll not say anything for now." With the sun setting, both groups decide upon a spot to spend the night, well secluded in a thicket, just outside a village. The afternoon had gone so smoothly they had passed through several villages quickly before reaching this one. They agree to take turns standing guard, for though it has been peaceful during the daytime, these people have a fear of the night: easy to understand after all they have been through in these past weeks and month.

In the middle of the night, Karin is awakened by the sound of a branch breaking just outside her side of the wagon. She arises quickly to see what's there. "Where's the guard?" she thinks, then just as quickly she peeks out an opening to witness a hand going over her Father's mouth, preventing him from yelling out on guard duty. She shouts a warning, and the whole group from both wagons is out, just like that. Sleeping lightly has become a way of life for these people, who rightly fear the night in the war-torn German countryside. "Help Father!" Jutte cries, and just that soon, the family man of the other wagon lands a devastating blow upon the unwelcome intruder. Jutte's Father wiggles lose, and just that quickly Mother is there with rope from the storage box; all take a hand in tying up this ruffian. But wait, this fellow is no ordinary ruffian, look at his outfit. He has all the padding of a pikeman.

"What are you doing here?" shouts Father, "You're a no-good plundering pikeman, you belong with your troops, wherever they are."

"I know, Sir. I need food and the village is too open to be seen. I would never escape there alive in this Catholic force attire. I saw your caravan and thought, here is an opportunity to get food, but then that branch broke under my foot, and I had to take action. I am sorry but I couldn't take the war anymore. I'm a soldier who ran away from Count Tilly's army after that last skirmish. He's headed north, just a few days from likely being here. Please, don't kill me, I mean no harm." Father and he look eye to eye; the securely roped intruder staring helplessly from the ground.

"We're not going to kill you, but tell us why you're headed away up here?"

"I left my horse over there, back of the oak trees, out of sight, down the hill, so I could come quietly in search of food. There's nothing left in the village we attacked, and not much is left to scavenge between here and there. It seemed the only hope was to head north, away from the worst of it, where maybe people would still have supplies. Things haven't been as bad up this way as yet. Then I saw this thicket, and the wagons, and decided upon the quiet approach to investigate. You know, not only the people are starving where

I have been, also the garrison of our troops is in dire straits. If I'm discovered by that garrison when Tilly moves this way, my life will not be worth anything. I'm a traitor. Here I am, on the ground, and when you gave me that look, and I stared back, I sensed a new life, a hope I haven't seen anywhere in many months. My Elector had been Lutheran until the Edict, then he compromised and became Catholic when it was forced. He wanted to stay in good with the Hapsburgs and Rome. He thought it better than risking conflict. We all had to become Catholic, along with Landgrave. That's how I ended up becoming a pikeman in Count Tilly's force. They found out I had skill in that position from my prior service in our local garrison."

All the families, including the men holding him down, felt a change in the spirit of things. This fellow seemed to mean it as he spoke from his desperate situation. An eye to an eye, a look to a look, and an uneasy support began to build between the intruder and his newfound people. "Alright," Father says, "We'll let you stay with us the rest of tonight, but you'll have to remain tied to our wagon till morning, so we can be sure you mean what you're saying. Jutte, go get this man some bread, then we'll return to our night's rest."

The rest of the night was quiet but uneasy. With the dawn the families arise to find a breakfast already prepared by the women, even the plundering pikeman now untied, through his trustful promise, has helped ready things for the meal, by gathering firewood and cooking a rabbit from the thicket. Talk continues among the group, each family and their surprise guest telling how they have changed colors quite a few times in their church attachments, to make it through this struggle so far in their various escapes. They have worn many coats of belief, while basically never changing underneath. Our family, Calvinists, the caravan-joining family

Lutherans and now this lone soldier, officially Catholic, turning coat back to his original Lutheran heritage.

"Got to get rid of these clothes," says the pikeman. "I'll never make it alive through this next village in daylight if they see me this way." Father looks through what he has, the man of the second wagon does the same, and together there's enough to spare to change the pikeman into a civilian. Our intruder, now an accepted part of the group, says he can lead with his horse. One more addition to the caravan seems quite all right. While the families are loading the wagons for the new day, the pikeman goes for his horse, tied up to the oak tree there over the hill (from the night before). All give a sigh of relief as he returns. This man "is for real." He didn't try to escape with his new set of clothes. He meant what he said, last night, notes Father, as the group readies the horses for the trip into the village. Off on the trail they go, with the horseman ahead, wearing a smile, and a bit of hope that things will better for him. He never wanted to leave his Lutheran faith anyway, and now he looks to new possibilities in some village that will accept him, perhaps with his new found friends.

Jutte and Karin look toward the village Plau as they are entering and Karin says, "I wonder what these people are like."

Jutte replies, "I know they're different that we are, because there's no destruction around here. They don't know war like we do, at least not yet."

"I hope it doesn't come up here," says Karin. Mother affirms that wish but conveys that since the Edict is set upon the whole countryside, no one is free from the potential invasion of the Catholic league.

"That's the sad part," Father interjects, "that's the reason we keep moving, for the Swedes have secured this northland for now, including the town of Rostock on the Baltic Sea, not too far ahead of us."

The group stops long enough to obtain some supplies at a market in Plau, bartering with the shop owner in trade of some items from their wagon to cover expense beyond their few remaining coins. Next the village of Karow, and it is here their caravan diminishes in size, for the Lutheran family, who joined them, finds a man they know. In the afternoon sun, the conversation goes on, including an invitation to join the Lutheran community. The Lutheran family accepts, but the Calvinist family expresses their wish to go on. It's a parting of ways. The families wish each other well. Both are glad they met in that fork of the road a day or so before. It's hard to find friends in the German countryside in these times, as people are so desperate no one places much trust in strangers, who might just turn out to be robbers in disguise. They still have the former pikeman with them, and he decides to continue on north with our Calvinist family. Good progress is made in this flat land toward the coast., as the wagon moves along at a faster rate. Now there are a few raindrops falling to help relieve the heat for the horses and family.

"It's cooler today," chimes in Karin, as the family anticipates arrival in Rostock. The lead horseman carries a good pace, which seems to encourage Father's horse to keep up. The wagon of travelers produces the best distance day of the whole escape.

"I wonder how John's doing," exclaims Father as all are gathered near the front of the wagon, enjoying the beautiful countryside.

"Why don't we live here?" replies Jutte, but then thoughts turn to the past, and all this country's going through, and even Jutte says, "Let's go on."

"John? I know he's doing well." Mother reassures the

family. All are thankful he's made a decision with the Swedes, that may well spell hope for their future, too.

It's evening, the longest journey since Hesse, and their leading horseman sees a good spot to put up for the night. "Rostock can't be far away now," Father whispers in a clear soothing voice to his family, as the wagon pulls off into a hidden area near a grove of trees.

"I'll keep guard for the first half of the night," says the former pikeman. The family agrees to share the second half. After a good late supper in the dark, a restful night begins. No intruders, no strange animals, and no more rain; just peaceful quiet to end a long successful day. It's fortunate for our travelers that this summer has been very dry with many days of sunshine along the trail.

With the dawn all are up with the sun. Jutte and Karin go to a spring-fed stream the family discovered last night, to wash and bring back fresh water. Our family has been blessed several times at their encampments, to find such a stream. Jutte carries a kettle from the wagon to pick full with berries growing along the bank. "These are nice ones," Jutte exclaims as she dumps a hand full into the kettle now held by Karin.

"Yes, I think so too; it's good we've found a place where everthing has not been trampled down by soldiers," replies Karin. "Now we have enough fresh fruit to last us until Rostock."

Back at the wagon a sense of peaceful trust descends upon the group as the pikeman reveals more about himself around the breakfast setting. Tears come to his eyes as he recalls how his fellow soldiers had raided a family's home for food, and when they refused, the four were strung up on their rooftop, and nailed down, and left to dry upon their housetop in the warm summer sun. "It tore my heart, but I didn't dare let on, or I could be their next victim. I suppose those four, parents and two children., will be skeletons upon that rooftop by next summer at this time."

"Oh my," says Jutte. "I never heard of anything so horrible."

"I know, says the pikeman," I could eat hardly anything, while the rest of the garrison gorged themselves on what was left in that house.

As the family readied their wagon for another day's journey, the pikeman revealed about his own family. "You people are so nice. I had family too, but when our Elector turned Catholic, they resisted and one by one they lost their lives as the Catholic League inspected our town and found them out. My Father was run through with a sword when he refused to give up one of his cows for army food."

The pikeman, more comfortable with them now, went on to tell about the plight of the rest of the family.

"My brother was dragged off to labor in an army uniform shop, and we never heard from him anymore, whether he is alive or dead. Finally my Mother and sister were severely beaten and left to starve after being taken away, for what the soldiers called 'lack of good work'. I'm the only one left, only for my skills as a pikeman, which the Catholic League found out about. It was join Count Tilly's force and save my skin, or be with the rest of my family in the grave, before my time. I chose to serve with Count Tilly and be a remnant of my family, and though my heart was not in it, I could buy some time, and hope for a better day."

"Wow!" Karin replies, "Now I can see what you're about, and I think you've made the best choice."

"We're on our way to Rostock," Father comments, "Stick with us if you will, for the rest of our journey north." With that invitation, the whole group continues on the trail in the morning sun. Through one village and the next, the day finishes within a short distance of the Rostock city boundary. Discussion centers on what they will do once they're inside the Baltic port city. Before the night's rest begins Father says he will need to go back to make contact with son John, after the family has settled in the port city. The pikeman offers to travel with Father to the Swedish regiment, when that time comes; nods of approval signify the family is happy with those plans.

CHAPTER NINE

With the break of dawn everyone is up, anxious to see what the city looks like. It's the first time to the Baltic coast for any of them. Father has heard about the Northern European University there, and all the culture these country folks have never seen. Jutte and Karin are in the wagon first. "Let's go" is their cry, and the enthusiasm spreads to everyone as they are on their way.

By midmorning, they are at the Rostock city boundary, with plenty of other people moving about, so they as strangers to the area are not really noticed; they sort of blend in with the rest. Keeping a sharp lookout, Father sees a church ahead. He shouts to their pikeman friend, turn left, I want us to stop here at this church and find out what we can about this city. With a quick dismount the pikeman ties his horse to a tree and assists Father as the wagon is pulled to the side and secured.

"Wonder if the parson is in today," replies Karin.

"I hope so; come on in," Father motions to his family. Inside the open door the group sees a room where someone is talking. As they round the corner an older lady greets them. Father says. "We're new here, is the parson in?"

"Yes, come on in," a bold voice proclaims, as into view comes the friendly face of the minister. Somehow a warm feeling comes over the whole group. How can anything bad arise with such a greeting? The entire family feels it. Mother gives a sigh of relief as Father begins to explain why they are here to see this man of the church. The older lady sees these people are in need of help, and offers to house them temporarily until further decision is made.

"I live alone in a big house. My husband died a few years ago. My family is gone, and right now I have no boarders residing in my spare rooms, so there's room for you people."

The pastor says, "What a great plan; you are Calvinists, like us, and I was just talking to the lady about what to do with her empty rooms, and you people walk in. We do have a sovereign and gracious God!" Discussion goes on about their willingness to work, and their hope for passage to Sweden. "Well, I'll help you look into possibilities in the coming days," says the parson, "but you know it will not be easy, for the war efforts take preference. The Swedes use this harbor quite a bit to support their troops here, as the King of Sweden advances to villages that need his help, and I hear it has really been bad down there in some places."

"Yes, we can tell you our experiences," notes Father. He proceeds to give tragedy after tragedy that has happened, including his own family events. "My son John is now serving in a Swedish garrison. I want to go and see him before we make any arrangements to leave the country. You know, my son has been so richly treated and influenced by the skills of King Adolphus and the Swedish army that he has accepted an offer to become a Swedish citizen."

"That may help," says the pastor. "That may help you

people in your passage across the Baltic Sea. But don't spread the word around here too greatly. The people here are not too gracious to those who flee from our homeland and fail to support the effort here, to keep us out of the clutches of the Catholic League. We fear the war could come up here too, and we want all our people here to stay, and band together if that time comes . . ."

"I understand," says Father, "we'll pretend we're new residents who have come to stay and protect your cause." Soon it's off to the older lady's home where provision is made for a protracted stay.

"This is a nice house," says Jutte.

"Thank you," comes the reply. "My husband was a professor at the University here in town. We had roomers who were mostly students, but now most stay at the University or close by and not here. Guess since my husband is gone, there is not as much attraction for the students to stay this far from the school."

"Oh," Karin retorts, "I think if I were a student I would want to stay here, with all these beautiful pictures and furnishings."

"We're grateful that you are willing to keep us," adds Mother. "We're just ordinary country folk and don't know about university life."

The older lady smiles, "You'll do fine and soon you'll be introduced to people who can help you. Now sit down, you must be tired from your travels. Enjoy this supper and then you can retire for a good night's sleep."

The next morning the older lady invites the village landgrave to her home to talk with our family. The full story pours out, as Father relates their experience. Contacts are made and arrangements are soon secured for work; sewing for Mother, cleaning for the girls, and Father will help at the ship dock, once he and the pikeman return from a visit to see son John. At this point, the family does not let on of their plan to leave the country.

From the information in town, it will be a three-day horse ride to the position where King Adolphus' troops are, so Father and the pikeman prepare the horses for a saddle back ride with enough provisions for themselves. The townspeople have been helpful to their new residents, and several people are there for the sendoff as the two men start their journey to see son John. The community is happy these people have a son serving in the Swedish army, for they may call upon that garrison themselves, in case of attack by the Catholic League.

It's over the flat lands to the south Father and companion go. First day, mostly abundant crops growing in the peaceful countryside, but by the second day evidence of war begins to show. There's sadness in the faces of both the pikeman and Father at the sight of trampled farmland where nothing grows, but only the record of turmoil, where some garrison has encountered another, or a village was plundered, deserted and left with the remaining people to starve. It' s a long story, the men have seen too often before and now it tears at their hearts as they ride along.

"We need to keep watch for troops," says the pikeman.

"Yes," replies Father, "we're getting into that area now." The next day a sight comes into their view which leaves the pikeman completely aghast.

"Look there," he says, "at that house in shambles. It's the one I told you about. Oh no! The skeletons are there, those four family members nailed to the rooftop." Both stop in awe. The pikeman leans against his horse, trembling. "It's awful! It's awful!" the pikeman exclaims. Father puts his hand on the pikeman's shoulder. He could see the thoughts of battle from the recent past were tearing him apart. Father himself had seen too much. The loss of brother Tom in Magdeburg returns to his thoughts, and the fire, it was horrible too, though they had escaped as a family of four, still alive and hoping for a better life. Somehow they had been blessed in a calico dance, between the tragedies, while this poor family, whose remains they view on the rooftop, didn't have that chance. It's several minutes before either one can compose himself enough to think what their next steps are. It's as though another reign of terror had come down upon them, like nothing they had been asked to bear before. As Father comes to his senses, he looks toward the face of the pikeman, who has just now opened his eyes again.

"Come on," Father says. "We must get on our way to find John." Soon, evidence of recent troop movement appears, fresh hoof marks, and over the hill into the next valley the pair actually spy the Swedish soldiers in the distance. Father receives a fresh burst of energy, knowing he's not far now from his son. Hope runs through his soul. How is son John, has he seen more battles, how are the troops doing? All those thoughts run through his mind, as he and the pikeman pick up speed. The horses gallop along now in a fast pace with Father urging at the reins. Soon they meet a lead garrison who are suspicious of these riders. Father and pikeman signal they mean no harm. The troops respect them and ask why they ride into this circle of soldiers, who are apparently about to start come training exercise on the musket range. Although these guns are crude and yet inaccurate in battle, King Gustavus has trained his fighters to be the best in Europe with these weapons. Combined with cannon, pikemen, and a few leftover knights in shining armor, the musketeers have found their place, in the success of the Swedish troops. They have become well-known throughout the countryside and villages for their vigor and prowess. These Vikings mean business, as the Catholic League was to find out in the battle of Breitenfeld. That battle was a turning point for the

Protestants who prevailed there in their greatest victory of the war.

I'm looking for my son, John, who is a musketeer in one of your garrisons."

"Oh," says the Swede, "I've heard of him; he's doing well. Go over the next hill and you'll find his garrison. Here, take this flag with you so there will not be trouble. The Swedish colors will get you in more easily." Father smiles, and nods in agreement, and mounts the flag on his saddle. It wasn't too long ago his family had mounted a Catholic flag on their wagon to get through a difficult situation, now he's pretending to be a Swede to see his son. This German is readily learning how to compromise, that's what it boils down to. Off the pikeman and Father ride, as fast as the horses are able, and soon the next horizon comes into view, with troops scattered about in the valley.

"Do you see him?" There's a larger group over there, near the woods. "There's my son," Father shouts, and soon there's a glad reunion. The pikeman takes the flag and displays it to the rest of the soldiers, so they know it's not trouble this group of travelers brings to the garrison. The Swedes are preparing to surround the nearby village which is in danger of attack from Wallenstein's army, and the visit must be short with Father and son. The pikeman explains to the leader of the garrison why they are here, while Father and John converse.

Back in Rostock the family has already experienced several days' work, and it's going well. Jutte and Karin work together cleaning houses of wealthy people near the university, where the older lady has many friends, and they are well accepted. Mother has been doing sewing in the older lady's home, work details from the local tailor's shop that she returns there to be sold. Supplies are being restored and new people are met, that may play a part in their future plans. All the family wonders how Father and pikeman are doing in their quest to find John. Life is more peaceful now, at least for awhile, a feeling this family has had little of in the past months since they left Hesse.

CHAPTER TEN

The Captain of the Swedish garrison provides a place for Father and John to talk during a morning break from musket target practice and troop maneuvers. All the details come out of what the family has done in Rostock, and how anxious they are to see son John before any escape to Sweden is attempted.

John comes up with an idea: "Father, I could see if the Swedish commanders would allow me to leave here and join you in Rostock. Perhaps if I agree to continue serving in the Swedish army, in another location, it will go well in receiving approval."

"That's up to you, son. We would certainly be happy if you could be with us as we set out to leave Mecklenberg Province." John rushes out of the tent to find the Captain, who happens to be conversing with other leaders of an adjoining garrison.

"Captain, could I speak with you for a bit?"

"What's your question?"

"I have a request, if you would consider it."

"Go ahead," as the Captain explains that John is one of his best leaders in the musket line of the garrison.

"Well, Captain, my family is in Rostock now, and hopes to sail for Sweden to start a new life there in a few weeks. Would it be possible for me to transfer to that area to be with them before they leave?

"John, we would really miss you here in the garrison for you have served well, with the battles and sieges we've had. You have been an inspiration to us with your bravery and valor. You would be sorely missed, but I have family too, back in Sweden, and when there is an opportunity to see them I seize it. I'll talk with the General and see if we come up with a plan to have you continue your service in the Swedish army, in that country, as your family hopes to sail there."

John rushes back to his Father and tells him a decision will be made this afternoon, about his future service as a soldier. "Father, I hope this works out, I miss Mother, Karin and Jutte so much. I want to see them as soon as I can, back in Rostock. If the General says no, I think I would leave the army, just to be back with you and them."

"Now son, hush with those words, you must think of your life and what you have accomplished here. It would not be wise to throw all that to the wind, and not have the security you have now as a Swede serving in this fine army."

"Yes, I hope the General says I can," replies John. What is only a few hours seems like a lifetime to Father and John as they nibble on lunch through the noon hour. The pikeman joins them as they eat and seeks to buoy them up, knowing that the Swedes, though they are strong, are good at heart. Though he has served with the German forces, he knows about King Gustavus Adolphus and his willingness to protect villages that come under attack. Surely this kind of spirit pervades the troops. He feels John chances to have that time with his family are pretty good.

It was nearly time to go back to maneuvers, when in comes the Captain. John, Father and pikeman nearly freeze in anticipation. Almost afraid to look up at the face of the Captain, the word comes out. John, your request is granted! John is hardly able to speak. This now seasoned soldier has to sit down, trembling as he speaks. "Thank-you. When do I start?

You can start your trip to Rostock immediately and report to our Swedish command there. Details will be in place by the time you arrive. We have papers to send with you to verify your Swedish citizenship and your services in this garrison. John, take care, we'll miss you, but you will be in good hands at Rostock. We're glad you'll continue in the Swedish army with likely service across the Baltic Sea, at least part of the time. We need good men like you to help train new recruits in Sweden. You are provided with a horse and supplies to accompany you on your return to Rostock.

Within an hour, all is in place. Father, John and pikeman begin their three-day trip back to Rostock, enjoying the warmth of the afternoon sun, helped by the glow of a cheerful feeling. Soon the family will be reunited, ready for a new phase of their plan, in escape from German conflict. Evening comes. They decide to camp near a village. Less likely to be attacked there at night by ruffians. Evidence of past warfare is all around. The pikeman decides he doesn't want to go back on the same trail as they came. He doesn't want to see that house again, with four dead people nailed to the roof. They will choose a slightly different route so that sorrow is not refreshed in his mind, to torment him through the rest of this trip.

As morning comes, off on a less traveled route they travel, and once out of the war zone, crops appear again. Life appears growing, without that stench of deadness which has so often been within the realm of these three. No wonder why the pikeman escaped; Father escaped, and John decided to become a mercenary soldier. Besides being driven out of their homeland, they couldn't take it anymore. Something had to give, and it was they, headed toward a new homeland. The day goes quickly, and they are well on their way back to Rostock, when they are met by a wagon traveling quickly toward them.

"Hello, where are you coming from so quickly?"

"Sir, we've been under attack, and we've only escaped with our lives and a few belongings. Most of what we had has been taken from us, by a band of soldiers."

"What soldiers were they, could you tell?"

"Well, I believe they were from Count Tilly. He has been advancing north but we didn't know he was this close. Guess there is a village up here that has been giving them a lot of trouble, not cooperating when the troops need food. They're about to put them under siege, I believe; you better be careful and keep an eye out on this trail. You know how savage the troops are, especially when there's no food."

"Yes, we know very well," replies Father. "Our family has been through a lot of that." With that, the wagon takes off again and is soon out of sight, wasting no time moving away from the trouble they had been in. Father, John and pikeman, heading the opposite way, pick up the gallop of their horses, hoping likewise to clear the area before sunset. The distance and the time go rapidly. They see there is evidence of troop movement in the area, probably where the visitors' wagon was attacked. They sneak through without any incident.

Encampment is made within less than a day's journey from Rostock. All fall asleep, comforted in the thought this part of their ordeal is nearly over. Even though the route has been a little longer in return, due to the pikeman's wish for a detour, these men have made record time with their horses. Apparently both man and horse felt the urgency to get back to Rostock.

With morning a quick start is made at dawn, right after a brief breakfast. "We should be back in Rostock by noon" says John. "I sure will be glad to see Mother and sisters again."

"I know, and they are eager to see you again, John. They want to tell you some of the plans we've made. Mother is working for a tailor, Jutte and Karin are cleaning for a wealthy lady."

"Father, I'll be glad to assist in any way, that I have time free to do, before troop assignment."

"I know son, you've already done a lot to help our situation."

Back in Rostock, work goes on diligently, however Mother and daughters anxiously wonder how Father, pikeman and John have gotten along. Did they find each other? Are they all right? Will they soon be back or has something befallen them on their return? It's been six days, everyone here has been nice, but it's the future, it's what they've been through and it has worn on them greatly, so that time seems like an eternity. Jutte pushes a broom right into Karin as she comes down the stairs of the house they are cleaning.

"Watch out, sister, you're in my way."

"Oh, Jutte, you never did watch closely, don't take things so hard, I know we're both on edge, but I know Father and John will be back today. I can feel it.

"I hope you're right, Karin."

The pastor and the elderly lady have been marvelous. They have helped Mother and daughters get acquainted at the ship dock, and apparently there will be a job waiting there for Father when he returns. Other than some frayed nerves, the morning goes as usual for the family, and, as they do each day, they return to the elderly lady's home for the noon meal. After eating and having discussion about plans for the next day, Jutte is first to step outdoors, for the return to work. One look down the street she notices three horsemen riding toward them. Could it be, could it be, she can't quite tell from a distance, but she goes running toward them. Yes it is! "Father! John!" she cries, and in a moment they are there, dismounting from their horses. She hugs both of them tightly. By that time Karin and Mother are there also, joining in the glad reunion. The pikeman leads the three horses to the house, while the whole family walks hand in hand back to the lady's home. The work afternoon will be shortened, for there is so much to say and do. Into the house they go for a roundtable discussion. The elderly lady relates to Father a job at the ship dock if he is willing to work there.

"Most certainly I will," he says, "that will be a good way to get acquainted with procedures there." John is to report to the Swedish authorities there too, perhaps we will get to know some ship's captain, to find when ships are scheduled to leave port." The elderly lady again cautions to be careful and disguise their plans to leave the country. Word has come just this morning in Rostock about that wagon which was attacked; the very one which Father, John, and the pikeman met on the trail. People are uneasy about it, for they know the war may be moving their way. They have rejected the restitution clause, and the church is not happy with their refusal to give up their Lutheran faith. Count Tilly is on the march and certainly they are on the list to be subdued by the Catholic League.

"We will be careful" says Father, "I will take a job there, pretending it is permanent. We'll act as though we're part of the community, ready to help in defense if Count Tilly comes here. The pikeman, at the table, offers what help he can be in these days ahead, but it is time for him to move on. He will also seek work in the city for the time being, then look for a more permanent situation, if there can be one in this turbulent county. After hugs, all say good-bye to him feeling their paths may meet again before they leave this Baltic port. The pikeman doesn't know if any of his family members remain, back in his village. It's not a place he wants to go back to, anyway, with all the sad memories, so he will just hope for a better life up here in this coastal area.

"You can count on us if you need help, while we're here," Father tells the pikeman. After a firm handshake, the former Catholic Leaguer in name only, steps out the door into the world ahead of him, as brave as any pikeman of the past, the family watching as he travels down the street.

"That is a good man," says Karin; John nods in agreement.

"We've all got our world ahead of us," Father exclaims, "let's be about this morning's work, while John and I go down to the ship dock."

Just then the pastor steps in the door. "Good morning, Madam!"

"What news do you bring us today?" queries the elderly lady.

"Well, I have both good news and bad news. The good news first. I've talked with the shipping people at the dock. There is a number of shipments going out next week to Sweden. They need extra people to work in preparation for that time, readying the cargo for the boats."

"Sounds like I have a job for sure," says Father.

"Yes, you do, I'll give you a recommendation. There will be no problem. However, I'm sad to let you know it will be extra difficult to leave the country on these boats, for the ships are not willing for passengers. Maybe John's citizenship will help, I'm not sure, however it will be best to seek passage at that time, for it is believed Count Tilly will certainly be here within two weeks, and who knows what conflict will occur if the Catholic League presses the issue of our rejection of their plan. It may not be safe here, or in boarding a ship."

A worried look crosses the faces of the family. Even here in tranquil Rostock, the war is creeping into their plans for escape. Even more determined for escape, they each set out on the day's activities, convinced a trip across to Sweden is the only way to rid themselves of this ongoing turmoil that has ruined their German homeland.

At the dock, both John and Father meet the Captain of a ship. The Calvinist pastor who first met our family when they arrived in Rostock, is a good friend of the Lutheran pastor who works often at the docks ministering to the Swedish sailors. Their relationship is a great help in getting quick information to the townspeople about troop movements. Our family is blessed by having each of these pastors to assist them at this time in their struggle.

He already knows of their arrival, for the Lutheran pastor had given him information before the two men appeared. Seems like things move quickly in this university town, even at the ship dock. Father is pleased with his new job, as he and the Captain soon get acquainted. John is sent to the Swedish command to find out how he will fulfill his requirements in the Swedish army.

"Hello, John, we're glad you're here. Your Captain sent word you would be arriving soon. You certainly have done well in your garrison. That battle experience near Brandenburg stands high in our estimation. Especially with your ingenuity taking across the moat to that stockade, with four of those local mercenaries helping you. That castle was completely overwhelmed. Your wisdom and bravery are just what we are looking for. We want you to be an instructor in Sweden training new soldiers who are coming up to replace those whose terms in Germany are nearing an end. You know the countryside there, and that will help as you instruct those new musketeers."

"Yes, I will be happy too. I do have one request however."

"What is it?"

"I have family who have escaped the turmoil of the war. They are up here in Rostock, hoping to go to Sweden also."

"How many are there?"

"I have two sisters, Mother and Father. All are now working here for as long as needed. Through the help of the Calvinist pastor and an elderly lady from the University they have jobs and housing for the time being."

"Are they citizens of Hesse?"

"That's right, but from all they have experienced and with my decision to become a Swedish citizen, in the last few months, I believe they are ready to change countries."

"Your citizenship will certainly help them from our side of things, John, but with the Germans, it will not be so easy, especially now that Rostock is under threat of attack. In fact, their escape will be illegal most likely and against what the Elector of Mecklenburg would want. Too many of the people have deserted and not supported the defense which the Protestant Alliance is trying to form. Perhaps we can sneak them aboard a ship when you leave, before the Catholic League brings a siege around Rostock, but it must be done carefully."

"I understand, Captain, I will tell them, and we will start making plans how it can be done." That night the family gathers around the supper table. Thoughts flow freely in anticipation of boarding a ship, sailing to a new land.

The elderly lady, who joins them as they finish their meal, has some helpful suggestions. "Why don't you wait till the weekend, perhaps on Sunday when none of you will be looked for at work? It will be easier then to move to the ship dock unnoticed, there the Lutheran pastor will come, late in the day, to minister to those deck hands who are of the faith.

With his help, you may make contact with the sailors who could help you become possible stowaways of a sort, amidst the shipping supplies. I believe that at that time you will be less likely to be caught. Now be careful not to spread the news of such plans to anyone around here, especially with Count Tilly near. The nerves of this city could erupt in something you would not like, we have had our experiences in the past, when *The Edict of Restitution* was first proclaimed. The thought of Catholic control again does not sit well in the minds of the people. If they think your family is disturbing their chances for independence, your hopes for a ship to Sweden could be dashed."

Meanwhile, son John is getting acquainted with the ship's Captain of the vessel on which he will sail as a Swedish soldier, to begin his work near Stockholm. He shows his recent documents proclaiming his Swedish citizenship along with his military identification which the Captain approves for his transport across the Baltic, set to happen within a few days. Now comes the wait for the weekend. Will all these things come together for John and his family? It's a tense few days. John does get back one evening to see them before departure time, and they compare plans.

"Maybe, just maybe," Father says, "we'll be able to sail together. I hope the Lutheran pastor can find a common ship for us."

""I hope so too," replies Jutte. "Wouldn't it be nice if we could escape here together."

"It certainly would," chimes in Mother. Jutte nods in agreement, and somehow the thought becomes a family determining motive, strong enough to drive them past obstacles which could do in those of lesser faith.

Saturday morning, what belongings the family can stow upon their person are sorted out. The kindness of the elderly lady shows through again, as she agrees to buy the horses and wagon, thus keeping their secret of departure away from any merchant in town they might try to sell them to. Now the family is ready for the move to the dock Sunday morning.

CHAPTER ELEVEN

A rrival at the dock is not as easy as planned, for in their walk, the family meets one of Father's friends who asks what they are doing with all those things on their backs, walking the city streets on Sunday morning. "Oh, we're just out finding a new storage place, to relieve the kind elderly lady of some of our things. We've felt it was burdensome for her to store all our belongings."

"Oh," replies the friend, only half-convinced by that story.

On toward the dock, Jutte hears a commotion down the street. "What are all those people so excited about, Father?"

"I don't know, but let's head off this other way, I know another path into the shipping yards where I work." Off they go in the new direction where they meet the Lutheran pastor who had been waiting for them.

"I'm glad you came this way, for there's trouble up town."

"Oh, Pastor, what is it?" states Father.

"It's a surprise advance by Wallenstein, with a regiment of troops. We didn't know he had been given authority to command again. Those Hapsburgs are desperate to hold the country, but we didn't think they would stoop to this. Wallenstein is not liked by them for all his failures. Some of his lead soldiers are ransacking the city, we fear a siege will soon be put around us. You better hurry to see the Captain over at the far dock. I've already spoken with him."

"Thank you, Pastor, come on Jutte, Karin and Mother, let's go quickly!" Huffing and puffing, picking it up at an even faster pace, the family heads across the shipping yards. Jutte can hardly keep up, being the one less physically inclined, but she tries, for all the family has plenty of experience escaping trouble, and she does not want to be left behind.

"Look," Karin says, "Some soldiers are running toward the dock. Come on, Jutte, don't lag behind."

"I'm trying, Karin, but this back load is heavy. OOPS!" Jutte cries, as her toe catches on a rock and down she goes. The family looks back, but already a soldier has caught up with Jutte.

"Where are you going in such a hurry?" he asks.

"Oh, I was going over to the ship's Captain, with my family; we're expecting friends to arrive there this morning."

"A likely story, I think you had better come with me, and we'll see what you people are up to. "

"No, I wouldn't, I have to be with my family. See, I have a cut on my leg, I need to have it bandaged."

"Up you, girl! You're in my command now." As the soldier grabs her arm, she tries to wiggle loose, but his grip is tight. His sword nicks her leg in the struggle, opening the wound to a greater depth, and blood runs freely.

"Let me go, you're hurting me!" By this time John has seen his family coming across the shipyard, both he and Father see the incident with Jutte and the soldier. They head quickly toward her. John grabs the soldier as he attempts to lift his sword. Father knocks it loose and ties his arms with rope

Mother has found amidst their limited belongings. It's enough to hold the soldier back, temporarily, while Father and John hoist Jutte, with her arms around their shoulders, limping to the ship dock. The sword did make a more serious wound of her leg, and Mother attempts to treat it as they walk. John, who has already secured official passage upon the ship as a Swedish soldier, motions to the Captain that this is his family and please allow them aboard the vessel. The Captain does not hesitate, seeing the trouble they're in. Questions can be answered later, for this dock will soon be put under siege, along with the rest of the city. With no ships going in or out for awhile, they must be off into the Baltic quickly.

"All aboard!" The Captain turns to Father and says, "Our Lutheran pastor has spoken about you. That's why I let you aboard with your son John."

Father acknowledges, with a thankful nod, while the ship's Captain quickly commands his crew to release the ship's ropes from the dock and begin sail.

"We don't have much money, but we'll do whatever is necessary to leave this German soil in its bitter conflict. I hope there's some way we can take care of this trip to Sweden with our son."

The Captain, now in a more relaxed moment with the ship moving safely away from the dock, says, "Yes, your family can become indentured servants in Sweden, if that is your wish to pay for passage. This is really not a ship for passengers, since it is for military supplies to support the Swedish army, but many people do pay for passage to other countries by becoming indentured servants."

"Yes! Yes! Captain," replies Father, "we'll be happy to take care of our passage in that way." By this time Mother and Karin have taken Jutte to a cabin of the ship where they can lay her down to treat that badly cut leg. Mother searches through their limited belongings to find enough cloth for a makeshift bandage. Tears are rolling down Jutte's cheeks, for it hurts.

"Now, now, Jutte, it will be better in a few days, I'm certain," assures Mother. With that Jutte lies back with her head upon a puffed up blanket, turned into a pillow, which Karin arranged from material she found in a storage closet on the ship.

Mother stays with Jutte, while Karin goes top deck to see what Father and John are up to. She joins them as they are looking toward Rostock, now becoming a distant point upon the horizon. It's a strange feeling to see that port disappearing before their eyes. It's a sinking feeling in their stomachs as Karin, John and Father glance at one another, trying to fathom what all this means for the future of their family. They are left with just that stomach churning emotion, at this point, for they can't really know what it means, except that they have escaped Germany with all five family members still alive.

After an eerie silence, Father turns to Karin, "Where's Jutte?"

"She's down in a cabin where Mother and I found a place to rest her, while we bandaged her leg. It is quite bad, but I'm sure she will be all right. Mother is with her."

"The Captain has told us we may need to become indentured servants to pay for this passage to Sweden."

"I'm willing to work, Father, You can count on me," says Karin. "I know Mother and Jutte will too. We spent a lot of time in Rostock cleaning houses and mending. We'll have it paid off in no time."

"Thank you, daughter, I know all of you will do fine. I have faith this new country will be right for us. Let's all of us go down and relay this news to Jutte and Mother." John agrees, though he must spend his time in training Swedish soldiers, he will have money from his work to help them in their expenses, till all is taken care of, so a new life can truly begin.

The family together, with Jutte feeling less pain from that wounded leg, agrees to share in the responsibilities the new life will ask of them. Mother says, "Think of all we've been through the last few months. It's a wonder any of us are still alive, only by the provident care of God has it happened." Conversation turns now to specific events, from Hesse, the Magdeburg fire, the surprise attacks along the trail to the north, till finally the painful boarding of the ship at Rostock. It's quite a memory. One they will not forget, and since it is Sunday, they all find a sense of worship coming on, as Father gets out the family Bible. Prayers and Scripture follow. All give thanks to God, and pray for their beloved in the German homeland, who must yet suffer greatly in the days to come.

The Captain is nice to them and invites them to share meals with the crew, as they all journey across the Baltic Sea, finding space between the bundles of this supply ship. Even Jutte is able to limp along, around the ship, with her bandaged leg. "Take care, Sister, we don't want you to fall again," advises Karin.

"I will, I just want to keep up with what the rest of you are doing."

A couple of days, and call is made to all of them to come to the top deck. "What is it, Father?" asks Jutte.

"I don't know, but we better follow the Captain's orders." It's early morning, but the sun's rays are high enough to view the distant horizon. A calm sea helps all look without the ship rolling back and forth, at what appears as a land mass.

"Yes," the Captain says, "there's your Swedish port. We should be there in several hours, if the wind picks up, and it should as soon as the sun gets a little higher."

John has joined the family by now, and all just stand there gazing at the distant horizon, wondering what it will be like to set foot on that distant shore, and the new life they will lead in a new country. They know little about it except for the Swedish soldiers they've met. A tear comes to Jutte's eyes as she asks, "What about Uncle Tom, and Cousin Elizabeth, who will never see this?" Sad faces appear on each of the family as she utters that question. "And what about Cousin Mary back in Eschwege; she must think we've deserted them, will we ever see them again?"

Mother replies, "We all feel that way, Jutte, but it's the life we've been given. It's the life most of our people back in Germany are living with. We can only hope that someday there will be peace in our homeland, and we don't know when that day will be." After a few more moments of quiet staring into the distance and the distant future of their lives, all go down to the crew's deck for morning breakfast.

CHAPTER TWELVE

After breakfast everyone moves to the top deck. Good, the wind has picked up, and the Swedish shore is now more visible. The Captain tells our family this is Trelleborg, our ship will port there. You will have time once we dock to meet a man who I think can help you.

"Danke" (Thank-you), says Father. "We appreciate what you are doing for us. It will be a great help to have someone there who can assist us when we reach the port." The Captain then turns to instruct the crew as they prepare to dock in about an hour. Excitement stirs through the family as they check through belongings, making ready for a transfer to new ground, a new life, and the wonder of their future.

Jutte asks, "Should we kiss the ground when we arrive, like King Adolphus did when he first touched our soil in Germany?"

"Why not, if you feel that way, Jutte," replies Mother. Who knows? The whole family may do the same thing, after all they've been through. A trickle of hope now pours through their veins with the sight of Trelleborg ahead of them.

The hour passes quickly, and with everything they have, neatly gathered into a pile, limited as it is, all five gather at the edge of the ship to watch it dock, with this city now fully in view. "Look at those buildings," says Karin, "and over there is the Viking fort the Captain was telling us about built over 600 years ago. Look at the palisades and towers around it. No one would dare attack them."

"Yes," replies Father, "the Viking King Harald Blue Tooth, who built it, must have really cared for his people's safety."

Within a few more kilometers, the ship touches dock. After the crew has secured the vessel, our famly, including their soldier son and brother, John, embark onto the platform. Jutte's leg still bandaged and sore, does not restrict her from doing her thing, as she kneels to kiss the Swedish soil. The rest of the family, feeling her gesture is sufficient for all of them, help her back to her feet.

It's only a few minutes until a man, who is able to speak Deutsch, approaches them. "The Captain has just told me about you people and what you need. Come with me, and I will show you what you should do to get your start. There is a German colony of Swedes who have already migrated to our land from the conflict you're coming from. You may choose to work out your indentured status among them, until you're ready to take on the full stature of residents here." As they walk along with their gracious host, to a wagon and team of horses, the man goes on to say, "Your son John will be able to contact the Swedish army officials in our town, for assignment. Likely something will be worked out so that you can see him from time to time, not too far from Trelleborg, because there is a training camp for musketeers just a day's journey from here."

Into the wagon, our family is off toward the city center with their new-found host taking the reins. They stop in front of a building where a Swedish soldier is standing. This is where John departs to begin his duty in the Swedish army. With hugs of farewell, the rest continue their journey out of the city "It's about an hour now to that colony of former Germans I was telling you about," says their Swedish host. "I know you can find lodging there for these first few days."

Soon a home appears that is different than the others they have seen along the path. It is a huge place with quite a few windows. The team of horses is steered into the lane by our family's guide. A row of trees looks great in the late summer sun. There are many cows in the field with several men tending the cattle as chore time is drawing near.

"This will be the best place for you if they can accept another immigrating family; these people have had experience getting other newly arriving Germans adjusted to life here," says the Swedish guide.

"It certainly looks nice with a lot of room for people to stay," replies Mother. The rest of the family agrees. They are greeted at the door of the home by a polite couple who tell them to come in. As soon as as our family begins to relate their reason for being there, the Swedish host winks at the kind couple who had met them at the door. It's like all this has happened before, and the host knows it. It's the story heard more than once in recent years from families escaping the conflict from the continent to the south.

The kind couple says "Yes, we have room for you and your daughters." Father and Mother smile; it's one burden removed from their shoulders. It isn't long before the conversation turns to the people living in the area. "They speak excellent Deutsch, like we are here around this table, for we are all German from a few years back. It will be good for you to start work here, helping different farm people, 'cause they will teach you how to speak Swedish like the rest of us."

Our family lends a hand in the evening chores once their Swedish guide leaves to return to Trelleborg. After a meal, the long day ends, and all turn in for a restful night's sleep. During the night, however, our family is awakened by a thunder clap. Karin jumps from the bed, her nerves on edge. It's been a long time since they've heard a thunder storm, and the girls are scared, thinking it to be a roar of a cannon, or the sound of a musket they remember hearing far too often before in their young lives. After the dry summer down south, it will take a bit of time to get used to a summer rainstorm. After all of the family realize it's not an attack from unwelcome troops, they settle down to finish a good night's rest.

The days move along, Karin and Jutte milking cows for area farmers, Father working in the fields of farms of German families, for autumn is not far away in this Northland, while Mother occupies herself by sewing for quite a few different people. They earn the money that will soon pay for their passage to Sweden. Once that is taken care of, they can begin preparing for their own plot of land, and so live in this colony of like-minded German people.

It's autumn before they see John again, but how things have changed! There's a noticeable happiness in this family gathering. The threats of violence have left, and although it takes time for nerves to heal, our family is much more relaxed, feeling life again is giving them great opportunitites in the Swedish countryside. All debts are paid, and Father has now secured a plot of land that some day may be their own.

Everyone is pleased with John in his return visit. He is advancing with the training aspect, and he has been given command of the instructing crew in the regiment that trains musketeers. John is generous to his family, part of the reason they have been able to pay things off so quickly.

What about their adjustment to the society? Well, Karin is the first to gain hold in the Swedish language, but the rest are not far behind. The colony of former Germans is a great help in their adjustment and it appears Swedish citizenship is right around the corner for the entire family. There's a church which serves the community, allowing for both Calvinists and Lutherans to share a building, some in joint worship service and some in their separate traditions.

Father does surprise the family one morning when he comes on horseback to deliver a message he has received in town from their homeland in Hesse. Usually his return from trade or other business is normal, but everyone today can see he is very excited as he walks through the doorway. "What is it, Father?" shouts Jutte. By this time Jutte's leg is well mended, although a scar will always be there to remind her of the scuffle she had with that soldier and his sword.

"Why, daughter, I have news for you. There's word from Hesse."

"Oh, how is it there?" asks Mother. All ears are attuned as he reads the letter, given to him uptown.

> [Word has gotten to us that you people now live in Sweden. We didn't like it at first, but now it seems you were the wise ones, though you lost everything back here. Father was injured in an attack and is not able to do much. I have most of the chores and care of the house to do. We're tired and hungry, but we do have our lives and property. Things have calmed down a bit for now. Our Landgrave has compromised with the Catholic Church. We do forgive you for running away. God willing, we may see you again.
>
> Your cousin, Mary]

"How did they find out about us, Father?" asks Karin.

"I think it happened when Swedish forces were in Eschwege late this summer. Word about our son John is pretty well known among the soldiers, and likely they told the townspeople about our escape from Rostock with John's help."

"That makes sense," chimes in Mother, "It would be good to get word back to Mary if we can." The whole family agrees. For a moment there is silence, as all think of the tragedy that has happened and continues to happen in their homeland.

Such is the life of this family which has turned greatly in the less than a year. They are not the unusual ones among the Swedish Germans. They share and hear very similar stories in the colony where they live, in the days ahead. It helps knit the whole group together, in support of their lives there in a new land. Somehow the pain of the past is a steppingstone into the future. It is a fact that there were many German families that migrated to Sweden in the 17th century.

Please read the epilogue that follows to see what your author says about those times in 17th century Germany. He gives his reasons for writing this book, and his understanding of what was involved in the tragic conflict of the Thirty Years War.

EPILOGUE

In 1618 the Thirty Years' War got its start when a revolt by the Bohemian Brethren was put down by Catholic forces in the Battle of White Mountain, near Prague. It was in this area Wallenstein originated. He was very wealthy, able to maintain a large army with the funds available to him. He was more or less hired by the Catholic Church to lead their cause as a general of favorable troops. However, he wavered at times, being sympathetic to the Bohemian revolt against the Church. He was almost a Protestant at heart, and Rome was not happy with him much of the time, except that he could maintain a large army with all his money. Things got so bad in their relationship with him, that one day officers went into his headquarters and ran a sword through him, ending Wallenstein's life.

Count Tilly's life ended early too, as he died from wounds suffered in battle. He was, however, a more effective servant of the Catholic cause, except that he could not always have enough troops on hand to be victorious in battle.

King Gustavus Adolphus was effective; inspirational to

his troops, doing much good for the Protestant cause in the German province, but he carried his mission further than originally intended, deep into German territory. He captured and raided a number of Catholic towns, whose villagers suffered greatly from the Protestant attack. The Swedish King advanced through Catholic Bavaria, hoping to keep a sizable buffer zone between the Roman-controlled area, and the Protestants to the north. He did have a kindness in his heart, respecting the requests of both Catholic and Protestant villagers who came to him seeking to retain their religious positions peacefully. It was, however, in the Battle of Lutzen, that he was killed by a musket shot in his back. It is not known whether he accidentally got in the line of fire from enemy troops, or if one of his own soldiers shot him in the back. The Swedes did go on to win that battle under new leadership.

There is a lot of truth in the story I have written. Though it is a fictional family, the events they go through in their escape are true for many people of the time. Most of the battles and sieges listed did occur though the exact chronological time when they happened may differ slightly from our account. Most of the areas through which this family travels were the more severe areas of war's destruction. Though nearly fifty per cent of the population of Germany was decimated at this time, some portions of the country and its people were almost totally destroyed, while other areas escaped with hardly any suffering or destruction. The Magdeburg area, through which this family travels, saw the worst tragedy of the war. That city was destroyed by the fire described in our story. The loss of life was terrible, with ninety-five percent of the people killed during that night.

This was such a long drawn-out war that soldiers became calloused, desperate, and hungry, raiding homes for food, and ransacking villages for any valuables they could find. Like the ruffians, who lurked along roadsides, many of these soldiers lost any sense of the value of life other than their own survival. The Edict of Restitution had failed miserably with neither side being able to gain an upper hand. It was evident something had to be done to save the people who were left, so the peace agreement was reached at Westphalia after five years of negotiation. Even after the Peace of Westphalia was signed in 1648, it was about five more years before the soldiers could be convinced the war was over and that they should stop raiding houses and killing people. The war had become so much a part of their lives and culture they knew no other way to live.

It was a long time after 1648 before the countryside and its remaining people began to heal. Slowly the population increased, and the farmland became farmable again, but a permanent scar was left upon this people that would not be forgotten.

The five-year period after the Edict of Restitution was implemented saw the most intense period of fighting. This is the reason I chose this time to write about our family's escape, coupled with the King of Sweden's invasion of the land. A similar story could be written about a Catholic family, who would have suffered just as greatly at this time, and I welcome someone to do that. I understand and appreciate both sides of this issue.

BVG